Praise for
New York Times **and** *USA TODAY*
bestselling author Brenda Jackson

"Brenda Jackson writes romance that sizzles and characters you fall in love with."
—*New York Times* and *USA TODAY* bestselling author Lori Foster

"Jackson's trademark ability to weave multiple characters and side stories together makes shocking truths all the more exciting."
—*Publishers Weekly*

"Jackson's characters are wonderful, strong, colorful and hot enough to burn the pages."
—*RT Book Reviews* on *Westmoreland's Way*

"The kind of sizzling, heart-tugging story Brenda Jackson is famous for."
—*RT Book Reviews* on *Spencer's Forbidden Passion*

"This is entertainment at its best."
—*RT Book Reviews* on *Star of His Heart*

Dear Reader,

It's hard to believe that *A Wife for a Westmoreland* is the nineteenth book in The Westmorelands series and the fourth book about the Denver Westmorelands. Time sure flies when you're having fun, and I've really had a ball bringing you stories about such gorgeous men and women.

I knew Derringer Westmoreland was going to be a challenge when he appeared on the scene in *Hot Westmoreland Nights*. Besides being a man too handsome for his own good and a man used to playing the field, he's ruggedly seductive and can talk the panties off any woman. He's also a man who believes in getting whatever it is that he wants, no matter what it takes to get it, and he's decided he wants Lucia Conyers. That would be all fine and dandy for Lucia, since she's loved Derringer most of her life, but she wants him to want her for all the right reasons and refuses to settle for anything less. So what does this Westmoreland man have to do to get the woman he wants? I think you're going to enjoy the results.

All the best,

Brenda Jackson

BRENDA JACKSON

A WIFE FOR A WESTMORELAND

To Gerald Jackson, Sr. My one and only.

To all my readers who are joining me
on the Madaris/Westmoreland Cruise 2011 this month.
Thanks for making it special and this book is especially for you!

To my Heavenly Father. How Great Thou Art.

Better a meal of vegetables where there is love
than a fattened calf with hatred.
—*Proverbs* 15:17

ISBN-13: 978-0-373-73090-2

A WIFE FOR A WESTMORELAND

Copyright © 2011 by Brenda Streater Jackson

Recycling programs
for this product may
not exist in your area.

www.eHarlequin.com

Printed in U.S.A.

BRENDA JACKSON

is a die "heart" romantic who married her childhood sweetheart and still proudly wears the "going steady" ring he gave her when she was fifteen. Because she's always believed in the power of love, Brenda's stories always have happy endings. In her real-life love story, Brenda and her husband of thirty-eight years live in Jacksonville, Florida, and have two sons.

A *New York Times* bestselling author of more than seventy-five romance titles, Brenda is a recent retiree who now divides her time between family, writing and traveling with Gerald. You may write Brenda at P.O. Box 28267, Jacksonville, Florida 32226, by email at WriterBJackson@aol.com or visit her website at www.brendajackson.net.

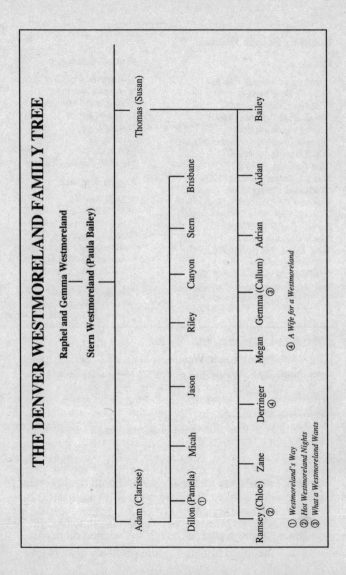

THE DENVER WESTMORELAND FAMILY TREE

Raphel and Gemma Westmoreland

Stern Westmoreland (Paula Bailey)

Adam (Clarisse)

Thomas (Susan)

Dillon (Pamela) ①

Micah

Jason

Riley

Canyon

Stern

Brisbane

Bailey

Ramsey (Chloe) ②

Zane

Derringer ④

Megan

Gemma (Callum) ③

Adrian

Aidan

① *Westmoreland's Way*
② *Hot Westmoreland Nights*
③ *What a Westmoreland Wants*
④ *A Wife for a Westmoreland*

One

Lucia Conyers's heart was beating like crazy as she made a sharp turn around the curve while the wheels of her SUV barely gripped the road. She knew she should slow down, but couldn't. The moment she'd heard that Derringer Westmoreland had been taken to the emergency room due to an injury he sustained after being thrown from a horse, a part of her had nearly died inside.

It didn't matter that most of the time Derringer acted as though he didn't know she existed or that he had a reputation in Denver as a ladies' man—although she doubted the women he messed around with could really be classified as ladies. Derringer was one of Denver's heartthrobs, a hottie if ever there was one.

But what did matter, although she wished otherwise, was that she loved him and would probably always love him. She'd tried falling out of love with him several times and just couldn't do it.

Not even four years of attending a college in Florida had changed her feelings for him. The moment she had returned to Denver and he had walked into her father's paint store to make a purchase, she'd almost passed out from a mixture of lust and love.

Surprisingly, he had remembered her. He'd welcomed her back to town and asked her about school. But he hadn't asked her out, or offered to share a drink somewhere for old time's sake. Instead, he had gathered up the merchandise he'd come to the store to buy and left.

Her obsession with him had started back in high school when she and his sister Megan had worked on a science project together. Lucia would never forget the day that Megan's brother had come to pick them up from the library. She'd almost passed out when she first laid eyes on the handsome Derringer Westmoreland.

She thought she'd died and gone to heaven, and when they were introduced, he smiled at her, showing a pair of dimples that should be outlawed on anyone, especially a man. Her heart had melted then and there and hadn't solidified since. That introduction had taken place a few months after her sixteenth birthday. Now she was twenty-nine and she still got goose bumps whenever she thought about that first meeting.

Ever since her best friend, Chloe, had married Derringer's brother Ramsey, she saw more of Derringer, but nothing had changed. Whenever he saw her he was always nice to her. But she knew he really didn't see her as a woman he would be interested in.

So why wasn't she getting on with her life? Why was she risking it now by taking the roads to his place like a madwoman, needing to see for herself that he was still in one piece? When she'd gotten the news, she'd rushed to the hospital only to receive word from Chloe that he'd been released and was now recuperating at home.

He would probably wonder why she, of all people, was showing up at his place to check on him. She wouldn't be surprised if some woman was already there waiting on him hand and foot. But at the moment it didn't matter. Nothing mattered but to make sure for herself that Derringer was okay. Even the threat of possible thunderstorms this evening hadn't kept her away. She hated thunderstorms, and yet she had left her home to check on a man who barely knew she was alive.

It was a really stupid move, but she continued to speed down the road, deciding she would consider the foolishness of her actions later.

The loud sound of thunder blasting across the sky practically shook the house and awakened Derringer. He immediately felt a sharp pain slice through his body, the first since he'd taken his pain medication, which meant it was time to take more.

Wrenching at the pain, he slowly pulled himself up in bed, reached across the nightstand and grabbed the pills his sister Megan had laid out for him. She'd said not to take more before six, but a quick glance at his clock said that it was only four and he needed the relief now. He was aching all over and his head felt as if it had split in two. He felt sixty-three instead of a mere thirty-three.

He had been on Sugar Foot's back less than three minutes when the mean-spirited animal had sent him flying. More than his ego had gotten bruised, and each and every time he breathed against what felt like broken ribs he was reminded of it.

Derringer eased back down onto the bed and laid flat on his back. He stared at the ceiling, waiting for the pain pills to kick in.

Derringer's Dungeon.

Lucia slowed her truck when she came to the huge wooden marker in the road. Any other time she would have found it amusing that each of the Westmorelands had marked their property with such fanciful names. Already she had passed Jason's Place, Zane's Hideout, Canyon's Bluff, Stern's Stronghold, Riley's Station and Ramsey's Web. She'd heard when each Westmoreland reached the age of twenty-five they inherited a one-hundred-acre tract of land in this part of the state. That was why all the Westmorelands lived in proximity to each other.

She nervously gnawed on her bottom lip, finally thinking she might have made a mistake in coming here when she pulled into the yard and saw the huge two-story structure. This was her first time at Derringer's Dungeon and from what she'd heard, most women only came by way of an invite.

So what was she doing here?

She brought her car to a stop and cut off the engine and just sat there a moment as reality set in. She had acted on impulse and of course on love, but the truth of the matter was that she had no business being here. Derringer was probably in bed resting. He might even be on medication. Would he be able to come to the door? If he did, he would probably look at her as if she had two heads for wanting to check on him. In his book they were acquaintances, not even friends.

She was about to back out and leave, when she noticed the rain had started to come down harder and a huge box that had been left on the steps of the porch was getting wet. The least she could do was to move it to an area on the porch where the rain couldn't touch it.

Grabbing her umbrella out the backseat, she hurriedly got out of the truck and ran toward the porch to move the box closer to the door. She jumped at the sound of thunder and drew in a sharp breath when a bolt of lightning barely missed the top of her head.

Remembering what Chloe had once told her about how the Westmoreland men were notorious for not locking their doors, she tried the doorknob and saw what her best friend had said was true. The door was not locked.

Slowly opening the door, she stuck her head in and called out in a whisper in case he was downstairs sleeping on the sofa instead of upstairs. "Derringer?"

When he didn't answer, she decided she might as well bring the box inside. The moment she entered the house, she glanced around, admiring his sister Gemma's decorating skills. Derringer's home was beautiful, and the floor-to-ceiling windows took full advantage of the mountain view. She was about to ease back out the door and lock it behind her when she heard a crash followed by a bump and then a loud curse.

Acting on instinct, she took the stairs two at a time and stumbled into several guest bedrooms before entering what had to be the master bedroom. It was decorated in a more masculine theme than all the others. She glanced around and then she saw him lying on the floor as if he'd fallen out of bed.

"Derringer!"

She raced over to him and knelt down beside him, trying to ignore the fact that the only clothing he had on was a pair of black briefs. "Derringer? Are you all right?" she asked, a degree of panic clearly in her voice. "Derringer?"

He slowly opened his eyes and she couldn't stop the fluttering of her heart when she gazed down into the gorgeous dark depths. The first thing she noticed was they were glassy, as if he'd taken one drink too many... or probably one pill too many. She then took a deep breath when a slow smile touched the corners of his lips and those knock-a-girl-off-her-feet dimples appeared in his cheeks.

"Well, now, aren't you a pretty thing," he said in slurred speech. "What's your name?"

"Puddin' Tame," she replied smartly. His actions confirmed he'd evidently taken one pill too many since he was acting as if he'd never seen her in his life.

"That's a real nice name, sweetheart."

She rolled her eyes. "Whatever you say, cowboy. Would you like to explain why you're down here and not up there?" She motioned toward his bed.

"That's easy enough to answer. I went to the bathroom and when I got back, someone moved the bed and I missed it."

She tried keeping the smile from her face. "You sure did miss it. Come on and hold on to me while I help you back into it."

"Someone might move it again."

"I doubt it," she said, grinning, while thinking even when he was under the influence of medication, the deep, husky sound of his voice could do things to her. Make the nipples of her breasts strain against her damp shirt. "Come on, you have to be hurting something awful."

He chuckled. "No, in fact I feel good. Good enough to try riding Sugar Foot again."

She shook her head. "Not tonight you won't. Come on, Derringer, let me help you up and get you back in bed."

"I like it down here."

"Sorry, pal, but you can't stay down here. You either let me help you up or I'll call one of your brothers to help you."

Now it was he who shook his head. "I don't want to see any of them again for a while. All they know how to say is, I told you so."

"Well maybe next time you'll listen to them. Come on."

It took several attempts before she was able to help Derringer to his feet. It wasn't easy to steer him to the bed, and she suddenly lost her balance and found herself tumbling backward onto his bed with him falling on top of her.

"I need you to shift your body a little to get off me,

Derringer," she said when she was able to catch her breath.

He flashed those sexy dimples again and spoke in a voice throaty with arousal. "Um, why? I like being on top of you, Puddin'. You feel good."

She blinked and then realized the extent of her situation. She was in bed—Derringer's bed—and he was sprawled on top of her. It didn't take much to feel the bulge of his erection through his briefs that was connecting with the area between her legs. A slow burn began inching from that very spot and spreading all through her, entering her bloodstream and making her skin burn all over. And if that wasn't bad enough, the nipples of her breasts, which were already straining, hardened like pebbles against his bandaged chest.

As if sensing her body's reaction to their position, he lifted his face to stare down at her and the glassy eyes that snagged hers were so drenched with desire that her breath got caught in her throat. Something she'd never felt before, a pooling of heat, settled between her legs, wetting her panties, and she watched his nostrils flare in response to her scent.

The air between them was crackling more than the thunder and lightning outside, and his chest seemed to rise and fall with each and every beat of her heart.

Fearing her own rapid reaction to their predicament, she made an attempt to gently shove him off her, but found she was no match for his solid weight.

"Derringer…"

Instead of answering her, he reached up and cupped her face into his hands as if her mouth was water he needed to sip, and before she could turn her mouth away from his, with perfect aim, he lowered his mouth and began devouring hers.

Derringer figured he had to be dreaming, and if he was, then this was one delusion he didn't care to ever wake up from. Feasting on Puddin' Tame's lips was the epitome of sensual pleasure. Molded perfectly, they were hot and moist. And the way he had plunged his tongue inside her mouth, devouring hers was the sort of fantasy wet dreams were made of.

Somewhere in the back of his lust-induced mind he remembered getting thrown off a horse; in that case, his body should be in pain. However, the only ache he was feeling was the one in his groin that signaled a need so great his body was all but trembling inside.

Who was this woman and where did she come from? Was he supposed to know her? Why was she enticing him to do things he shouldn't do? A part of him felt that he wasn't in his right mind, but then another part didn't give a damn if he was in his wrong mind. The only thing he knew for sure was that he wanted her. He could eat her alive and wouldn't mind testing that theory to see if he really could.

He shifted his body a little and brought her in the center of the bed with him. He lifted his mouth only slightly off hers to whisper huskily against her moist lips, "Damn, Puddin', you feel good."

And then his mouth was back on hers, sucking on her tongue as if he was a man who needed to taste her as much as he needed to breathe, and what was so shocking to him at that moment was that he was convinced that he did.

* * *

Lucia knew she had to put a stop to what she and Derringer were doing. He was delirious and didn't even know who she was. But it was hard to stop him when her body was responding to everything he was doing to it. Her mouth had never been kissed like this before. No man had consumed her with so much pleasure for her not to think straight. Never had she known a woman could want a man with such magnitude as she wanted Derringer. She had always loved him, but now she wanted him with a need that had been foreign to her.

Until now.

"I want you, Puddin'…"

She blinked as he slightly leaned up off her and the reality of the moment hit her. Although he was delusional, Lucia realized that the honorable part of Derringer would not force her into doing anything she didn't want to do. Now was her chance to slide from beneath him and leave. Chances were, he wouldn't even remember anything about tonight.

But something wouldn't let her flee. It kept her rooted in place as she stared up at him, caught in a visual exchange that not only entrapped her sight but also her mind. A part of her knew this would be the one and only time she would have his attention like this. Sadly, it would be the one and only time he would want her. She pushed to the back of her mind that it had taken an overdose of pain medication to get him to this state.

If she didn't love him so much, she probably would have been able to fight this sexual pull, but love combined with lust was a force she couldn't fight, and a part of her truly didn't want to. She would be thirty in ten months and as of yet, she hadn't experienced how it would feel to be with a man. It was about time she did and it might as well be with the one and only man she'd ever loved.

She would take tonight into her soul, cradle it in her heart and keep it safe in the deep recesses of her brain. And when she saw him again she would have a secret he wouldn't know about, although he would have been the main person responsible for making it happen.

Captured by his deep, dark gaze, she knew it was only a matter of minutes before he took her silence as consent. Now that she'd made up her mind about what she wanted to do, she didn't want to wait even that long. And as more liquid heat coiled between her legs, she lifted her arms to wrap around his neck and tilted her mouth to his. The moment she did, pleasure between them exploded and plunged her into a mirage of sensations that she'd never even dreamed about.

He began kissing her senseless and in her lust-induced mind she was barely aware of him pulling her blouse over her head and removing her lace bra from her body. But she knew the exact moment he latched on to a nipple and eased it between heated lips and began sucking on it as though it was just for his enjoyment.

Waves of pleasures shot through every part of her as if she'd been hit with an atomic missile that detonated on impact. She caught his head between her hands to keep his mouth from going anywhere but on her. Several moans she hadn't known she was capable of making eased from her lips and she couldn't help but writhe the lower part of her body against him, needing to feel the hardness of his erection between her thighs.

As if he wanted more, she knew the moment his fingers eased up her skirt and tracked their way to the part of her that was burning more than any other part—her moist, hot center. He slid one hand beneath the edge of her panties and, as if his finger knew exactly what it was after, it slowly and diligently trekked toward her throbbing clitoris.

"Derringer!"

Her entire body began trembling and with all the intent of a man on a mission he began stroking her with fingers that should be outlawed right along with his dimples. Her womanly core was getting more attention than it had ever gotten before, and she could feel sensations building up inside her at such a rapid rate she was feeling dizzy.

"I want you," he said in a low, guttural tone. And then he kissed her again in a deep, drugging exchange that had him sliding his tongue all over her mouth, tasting her as if doing so was his right. Just the thought made her powerless to do anything other than accept his seduction with profound pleasure.

She was so into the kiss that she hadn't realized he had worked his briefs down his legs and had removed her panties, until she felt them flesh to flesh. His skin felt hot against hers and the iron-steel feel of his thighs resting over hers was penetrating through to every pore in her body.

And when he broke the kiss to ease his body over hers, she was so overcome with desire that she was rendered powerless to stop him.

He lowered his eyes to her breasts and smiled before his eyes slowly returned to her face and snagged her gaze. The look he gave her at that moment was so sexual that she was willing to convince herself that she was the only woman on earth he'd ever given it to. And she was just that far gone to believe it.

Then he leaned down and captured her mouth at the same time he thrust into her body. She couldn't help but cry out from the pain and, as if he sensed what had happened and just what it meant, his body went completely still. He eased his mouth away from hers and glanced down at her while still deeply embedded within her. Not sure just what thoughts were going through his mind about her virginal state and not really wanting to know, she reached up and wrapped her arms around him. And when she began using her tongue to kiss him the way he'd done to her earlier, she felt his body tremble slightly before he began moving inside her. The first time he did so, she thought she would come apart, but as his body began thrusting into hers, smoldering heat from him was being transferred to her, building a fire she could not contain any longer.

He released her mouth long enough for her to call his name. "Derringer!"

He was devouring her in a way she'd never been devoured before and she couldn't help but cry out as his tongue took over. The lower part of him was sending waves of pleasure crashing through her that had her sucking in sharp breaths.

She had heard—mainly from Chloe during one of their infamous girl chats—that making love to a man, especially one you loved, was a totally rewarding and satisfying experience. But no one told her that it could be so mind-consuming and pleasurable. Or that it could literally curl your toes. Maybe Chloe had told her these things and she hadn't believed her. Well, now she believed. And with each hard plunge into her body, Derringer was making all the fantasies she'd ever had of him a reality.

He released her mouth to look down at her while he kept making love to her, riding her the way he rode those horses he tamed. He was good. And he was also greedy. To keep up with him, she kept grinding her hips against his as sensations within her intensified to a degree that she knew she couldn't handle much longer. She cried out again and again as sensations continued to spiral through her.

And then something happened that had never happened to her before and she knew what it was the moment she felt it. He drove deeper and deeper into her, riding her right into a climax of monumental proportions. He lifted his head and met her gaze and the dark orbs gazing at her pushed her even more over the edge.

And when he whispered the name Puddin', thinking it was hers, she accepted it because it had sounded so good coming from him, and it was all she needed to hear to push her into her very first orgasm.

"Derringer!"

He lowered his head again and his tongue slid easily inside her mouth. She continued to grind against him, accepting everything he was giving. Moments later, after breaking off the kiss, he threw his head back and whispered the name again in a deep guttural tone, and he continued to stroke her into sweet oblivion.

* * *

Lucia slowly opened her eyes while wondering just how long she'd slept. The last thing she remembered was dropping her head onto the pillow. She'd been weak, spent and totally and thoroughly satisfied after making love to the sexiest man to walk the face of the earth.

He was no longer on top of her, but was asleep beside her. She missed the weight of him pressing down on her. She missed how his heart felt beating against hers, but most of all she missed the feel of him being inside her.

Remnants of ecstasy were still trickling through her when she thought of what they'd done and all they'd shared. Being gripped in the throes of orgasm after orgasm for several long moments was enough to blow anybody's mind and it had certainly done a job on her. And the way he had looked down at her—during those times he wasn't kissing her—had sent exquisite sensation after exquisite sensation spiraling through her. Even with the bandages covering his chest and parts of his back, she had felt him—the hardness of his shoulders and the way the muscles in his back had flexed beneath her fingertips.

There was no way she could or would forget tonight. It would always be ingrained in her memory despite the fact that she knew he probably would not remember a single thing. That thought bothered her and she fought back the tears that threatened her eyes. They should be tears of joy and not of sorrow, she thought. She had loved him for so long, but at least she had these memories to cherish.

The rain had stopped and all was quiet except the

even, restful sound of Derringer's breathing. Day was breaking and she had to leave. The sooner she did so the better. She could just imagine what he would think if he woke and found her there in bed with him. Whatever words he might say would destroy the beautiful memories of the night she intended to keep.

And her guess was that someone—any one of his brothers, sisters or cousins—might show up any minute to check up on him. They, too, would be shocked as heck to find her there.

She slowly eased out of bed, trying not to wake him, and glanced around for her clothes. She found all the items she needed except for her panties. He had taken them off her while she was in bed, so chances were they were somewhere under the covers.

She slowly lifted the covers and saw the pair of pink panties were trapped beneath his leg. It would be easy enough to wake him and ask him to move his leg so she could get them, but there was no way she could do such a thing. She stood there a moment, hoping he would stir just a little so she could pull them free.

Lucia nervously gnawed on her bottom lip, knowing she couldn't just stand there forever, so she quietly began getting dressed. And only when the sun began peeking over the horizon did she accepted that she had to leave quickly…without her panties.

Glancing around the room to make sure that was the only thing she would be leaving behind, she slowly tiptoed out of the room, but not before glancing over her shoulder one last time to look at Derringer. So this was how he looked in the early mornings. With his shadowed face showing an unshaven chin while lying on the pillow, he looked even more handsome than he'd been last night.

He would probably wonder whose panties were left in his bed, but then he might not. He bedded so many women that it wouldn't matter that one had left a pair of their panties behind. To him it might not be any big deal. Probably wouldn't be.

Moments later while driving away, she glanced back in her rearview mirror at Derringer's home, remembering all that had taken place during the night in his bedroom. She was no longer a virgin. She had given him something she had never given another man, and the only sad part was that he would never, ever know it.

Two

Some woman had been in his bed.

The potent scent of sex brought Derringer awake, and he lifted his lids then closed them when the sunlight coming through his bedroom window nearly blinded him. He shifted his body and then flinched when pain shot up one of his legs at the same time his chest began aching.

He slowly lifted his head from the pillow, thinking he needed to take some more pain pills, and dropped it back down when he remembered he might have taken one too many last night. Megan would clobber him for taking more than he should have, but at least he'd slept through the night.

Or had he?

He sniffed the air and the scent of a woman's perfume and of sex was still prevalent in his nostrils. Why?

And why were clips of making love to a woman in this very bed going through his brain? It was the best dream he'd had in years. Usually a dream of making love to a woman couldn't touch the reality, but with the one he'd had last night, he would beg to differ. He could understand dreaming about making love to a woman because it had been a while for him. Getting the horse business off the ground with his brother Zane, his cousin Jason and their newfound relatives, those Westmorelands living in Georgia, Montana and Texas, had taken up a lot of his time lately. But his dream had felt so real. That was one hell of an illusion.

Nevertheless, he thought, stretching his body then wishing he hadn't when he felt another pain, it had been well worth the experience.

He reached down to rub his aching thigh, when his hand came in contact with a lacy piece of material. He brought up his hand and blinked when he saw the pair of lace bikini panties that carried the feminine scent he had awakened to.

Pulling himself up in bed, he studied the underthings he held in his hand. Whose were they? Where had they come from? He sniffed the air. The feminine scent was not only in the panties but all over his bed as well. And the indention on the pillow beside him clearly indicated another head had been there.

Monumental panic set in. Who the hell had he made love to last night? Since now there was no doubt in his mind he'd made love to someone. All that pleasure hadn't been a figment of his imagination, but the real thing. But who had been the woman?

He closed his eyes and tried to come up with a face

and couldn't. It had to have been someone he knew; otherwise, who would have come to his house and gotten into his bed? He had messed around with some pretty brazen women in his lifetime, but none would have dared.

Hell, evidently one had.

He opened his eyes and stared at the wall, trying to recall everything he could about yesterday and last night. He remembered the fall off Sugar Foot's back; there was no way he could forget that. He even remembered Zane and Jason rushing him to the emergency room and how he'd gotten bandaged up and then sent home.

He definitely recalled how his brother and cousin kept saying over and over, "We told you so." He remembered that after he'd gotten into bed, Megan had stopped by on her way to the hospital where she worked as an anesthesiologist.

He recalled when she'd given him his pain medicine with instructions of when to take it. The pain had come back sometime after dark and he'd taken some of the pills.

Hell, how much of the stuff had he taken? He distinctly recalled the E.R. physician's warning that the painkillers were pretty potent stuff and had to be taken when instructed. So much for that.

Okay, so he had taken more pain medicine than he was supposed to. But still, what gave some woman the right to enter his home and take advantage of him? He thought of several women who it could have been; anyone who might have heard about his fall and decided to come over and play nursemaid. Only Ashira would have been bold enough to do that. Had he slept with her last night? Hell, he sure hoped not. She might try to pull something and he wasn't in the market of being any baby's daddy any time soon. Besides, what he'd shared with his mystery woman had been different from anything he'd ever shared with Ashira. It had been more profound with one hell of a lasting effect.

He then remembered something vital. The woman he'd slept with had been a virgin—although it was hard to believe he could remember that, he did. And it was pretty far-fetched to think there were still any of them around in this day and time. But there was no way in hell he could have imagined her innocent state even with a mind fuzzy with painkillers. And he knew for certain the woman could not have been Ashira since she didn't have a virginal bone in her body. Besides, he had a steadfast rule to leave innocents alone.

Derringer sighed deeply and wished, for his peace of mind, that he could remember more in-depth details about last night, including the face of the woman whose virginity he had taken. The thought of that made him cringe inside because he knew for certain he hadn't used a condom. Was last night a setup and the result would be a baby just waiting to be born nine months from now?

The thought of any woman taking advantage of him that way—or any way—made his blood boil. And anger began filling him to a degree he hadn't known was possible. If the woman thought she had gotten the best of him she had another thought coming. She had not only trespassed on his private property, but she had invaded his privacy and taken advantage of him when he'd been in a weakened, incoherent state.

If he had to turn over every stone in Denver, he would

find out the identity of the woman who'd had the nerve to pull one over on him. And when he found her, he would definitely make her pay for her little stunt.

"Lucia, are you all right?"

It was noon and Lucia was sitting behind the desk of her office at the Denver branch of *Simply Irresistible*, the magazine designed for today's up-and-coming woman.

The magazine, Chloe's brainchild, had started out as a regional publication in the Southeast a few years ago. When Chloe had made the decision to expand to the West and open a Denver office, she had hired Lucia to manage the Denver office.

Lucia loved her job as managing editor. Chloe was editor in chief, but since her baby—a beautiful little girl named Susan—was born six months ago, Chloe spent most of her time at home taking care of her husband and daughter. Lucia had earned a business-management degree in college, but when Chloe had gotten pregnant she had encouraged Lucia to go back to school and get a master's degree in mass communications to further her career at *Simply Irresistible*. Lucia only needed a few more classes to complete that degree.

Lucia figured it would only be a matter of time before Chloe and Ramsey decided they would want another baby, and the running of *Simply Irresistible's* Denver office would eventually fall in her lap.

"Lucia!"

She jumped when Chloe said her name with a little more force, getting her attention. "What? You scared me."

Chloe couldn't help but smile. It had been a long time

since she'd seen her best friend so preoccupied. "I was asking you a question."

Lucia scrunched up her face. "You were?"

"Yes."

"Oh, what was your question?"

Chloe shook her head, smiling. "I asked if you were all right. You seem preoccupied about something and I want to know what. Things are looking good here. We doubled our print run for April's issue since the president is on the cover, so that shouldn't cause you any concern. What's going on with you?"

Lucia nibbled on her bottom lip. She needed to tell someone about what happened last night and since Chloe was her best friend, she would be the logical person. However, there was a problem with that. Chloe was married to Ramsey, who was Derringer's oldest brother. There was no doubt in Lucia's mind Chloe would keep her mouth closed about anything if she asked her to, but still…

"Okay, Lucia, I'm only going to ask you one more time. What's wrong with you? You've been acting spaced out since I got here, and I doubt you were listening to anything Barbara was saying during the production meeting. So what's going on with you?"

Lucia breathed in deeply. "It's Derringer."

Frowning, Chloe stared. "What about Derringer? Ramsey called and checked on him this morning and he was doing fine. All he needed was a dose of pain medication and a good night's sleep."

"I'm sure he got the dose of pain medication, but I don't know about the good night's sleep," Lucia said drily, before taking a long sip of cappuccino.

"And why don't you think he got a good night's sleep?"

Lucia shrugged, started to feign total ignorance to Chloe's question and then decided to come clean. She looked up and met her friend's curious gaze.

"Because I spent the night with him and I know for certain we barely slept at all."

She could tell from the look that suddenly appeared on Chloe's face that she had shocked her friend witless. Now that she had confessed her sins, she was hoping they could move on and talk about something else, but she should know better than to think that.

"You and Derringer finally got together?" Chloe asked. The shocked expression had been replaced by a smile.

"Depends on what you mean by got together. I'm no longer a virgin, if that's what you mean," Lucia said evenly. "But he was so over the top on painkillers he probably doesn't remember a thing."

The smile dropped from Chloe's lips. "You think so?"

"I know so. He looked right in my face and asked me for my name."

She took the next ten minutes and told Chloe everything, including the part about the panties she had left behind. "So that's the end of it," Lucia finished her tale by saying.

Chloe shook her head. "I really don't think so for two reasons, Lucia. First, you're in love with Derringer and have been for a very long time. I don't see that coming to an end any time soon. In fact, now that the two of you have been intimate, you're going to see him in a whole new light. Whenever you run into him, your hunger for him will automatically kick in."

Chloe's expression became even more serious when she said, "And you better hope Derringer doesn't find your panties. If he does find them and can't remember the woman he took them off of, he will do everything in his power to track her down."

Lucia preferred not hearing that. She gripped the handle of her cup tightly in her hand. Turning away to look out the window to view downtown Denver, she drew in a deep ragged breath before taking a sip of her coffee. She hoped Chloe was wrong. The last thing she needed was to worry about that happening.

"With his reputation with women it will be like looking for a needle in a haystack."

"Possibly. But what happens if he finds that needle?"

Lucia didn't want to think about that. She had loved Derringer secretly for so long, she wasn't sure she wanted that to change, especially when he didn't love her back.

"Lucia?"

She turned and looked at Chloe. There was a serious expression on her best friend's face. "I don't know what will happen. I don't want to think that far. I want to believe he won't remember and let it go."

A few moments passed. "What I said earlier was true. Whenever you see Derringer, you're going to want him," Chloe said softly.

She shrugged. "I've always wanted him, Clo."

"Now it will be doubly so."

Lucia opened her mouth to deny Chloe's words and

decided not to waste her time because she knew Chloe was probably right. She had thought about him all that day, barely getting any work done. She kept playing over and over in her mind just what the two of them had done together. "I will fight it," she finally said.

Chloe bristled at her words. "It won't be that simple."

She could believe that. Nothing regarding Derringer had ever been simple for her. "Then what do you suggest I do?" Lucia said with resignation in her voice.

"Come out of hiding once and for all and go after him."

She wasn't surprised Chloe would advise her to do something like that. Her best friend was the daring one. She never hesitated in going after anything she wanted and she'd always envied Chloe for being so bold and brave.

Chloe must have seen the wistful look in her eyes and kept pushing. "Go after him, Lucia. Go ahead and take Derringer on. After last night, don't you think it's about time you did?"

A week later, Jason Westmoreland glanced over at his cousin and grinned. "Was that supposed to be a trick question or something?"

Derringer shook his head as he eased back in the chair. He'd done nothing over the past few days but stay on his pain medication and get plenty of sleep. Each time he awoke he would reach under his pillow and pull out the panties he had placed there just to make sure he hadn't dreamed the whole thing. They proved that he hadn't. And the name Puddin' Tame, the alias the woman had given him, kept going through his mind.

This morning he woke feeling a whole lot better and decided to lay off the pills. He hoped clearing his head would trigger something in his memory about what happened a week ago. So far it hadn't.

Jason had dropped by to check on him and the two were sharing early-morning coffee at the kitchen table. "No, it's not a trick question. I figured I'd ask you first before moving on to Riley, Zane, Canyon and Stern. Afterward, I'll compare everybody's answers."

Jason inclined his head with the barest hint of a nod. "Okay, I'll give your question a shot, so go ahead and repeat it to make sure I heard you right."

Derringer rolled his eyes and then leaned closer to the table. His expression was serious. "What can you tell about a woman from the panties she wears, both style and color?"

Jason rubbed his chin a moment. "I would have to say nothing in particular unless they are white, granny-style ones."

"They aren't." He hadn't told Jason why he was asking, and Jason, the easygoing Westmoreland, wouldn't ask... There was no doubt in Derringer's mind that everyone else would.

"Then I really don't know," Jason said, taking a sip of his coffee. "I think some pieces of clothing are supposed to convey messages about people. I picked white because it usually means innocence. But then again, Fannie Nelson had on a pair of low-riding jeans one day that showed her white panties, and she is a long way from being innocent."

"Aren't you curious as to why I want to know?"

"Yes, I'm curious, but not enough to ask. I figure you have your reasons and I don't want to come close to thinking what they might be."

Derringer nodded, understanding why Jason felt that way. His cousin knew his history with women. And what Jason said was true. He had his reasons, all right.

"So what do you plan to do today now that you've returned to the world of the living? I heard the E.R. doc tell you to take it easy for at least a week or so to recuperate, so you're still under restrictions," Jason reminded him.

"Yes, but I'm not restricted from driving. I'm going to hang around here and take it easy for a few more days before venturing out anywhere."

"I'm glad you're following the doc's advice. Although things could have been worse, that was still a nasty fall you took. And as far as your question regarding women's undergarments, I suggest you talk to Zane when he gets back from Boulder." Jason chuckled and then added, "And be prepared to take notes."

Two days later Derringer left home for the first time since his accident and drove to Zane's Hideout. He was glad to see his brother's truck parked in the yard, which meant he was back. Jason was right. He should have been prepared to take notes. Zane, who was only fourteen months older but a heck of a lot wiser where women were concerned, had no qualms about telling him what he wanted to know.

According to Zane, the color and style of a woman's panties said a lot about her. Sexually liberated women wore thongs or barely-there panties, all colors except white, and they rarely wore pastel colors. Most of them preferred black.

Zane further went on to say that women who liked to tease men wore black lace. Women who preferred lace to any other design were women who liked to look and feel pretty. And bikini panties weren't as popular these days as thongs and hipsters, so a woman still wearing bikini panties weren't as sexually liberated as others.

Derringer smiled when Zane, with a serious look on his face, advised him to steer clear of women who wore granny panties. Zane furthermore claimed that women who wore red panties gave the best blow jobs. Those with yellow panties the majority of the time weren't afraid to try anything and were pretty good with a pair of handcuffs. Blue panties–wearing women were loyal to a fault—although they had a tendency to get possessive sometimes, and those who preferred wearing green were only after your money, so the use of double condoms was in order.

It had taken his brother almost an hour to make it to pink panties and, according to the Laws of Zane, women who wear pink panties were the ones you needed to stay away from because they had the word *marriage* written all over them, blasting like neon lights. They were a cross between innocent and a woman with an inner hunger for getting laid. But in the end she would still want a wedding ring on her finger.

"Okay, now that you've taken up more than an hour of my time, how about telling me why you're so interested in a woman's panties," Zane said, eyeing him curiously.

For a moment Derringer considered not telling his brother anything, but then thought better of it. He, his five brothers and all his cousins were close, but there was a special bond between him, Zane and Jason. Besides, it was evident that Zane knew a lot more about women than he did, so maybe his brother could give him some sound advice about how to handle what had occurred that night, just in case he had been set up.

"Some woman came over to my place the night I was injured and let herself in. I can't remember who she was, but I do remember making love to her."

Zane stared at him intently for a moment. "Are you absolutely sure you made love to her and didn't imagine the whole thing? When we took you home from the hospital—right before I had to take off for the airport—you were pretty high on those pain meds. Megan figured that you would probably sleep through most of the night, although she set out more medicine for you to take later."

Derringer shook his head. "Yeah, I was pretty drugged up, but I remember making love to her, Zane. And to prove I didn't dream the whole thing, I found her panties in bed with me the next morning." What he decided not to say was that as far as he was concerned, it had been the best lovemaking he'd ever experienced with a woman.

Zane drew in a deep breath and then said on a heavy sigh. "You better hope it wasn't Ashira. Hell, man, if you didn't use a condom she would love to claim you're her new baby's daddy."

Derringer rubbed the ache that had suddenly crept into his temples at the thought. "It wasn't Ashira, trust me. This woman left one hell of an impression. I've never experienced lovemaking like it before. It was off the charts. Besides, Ashira called a few days after hearing about the accident. She left town to go visit her sick grandmother in Dakota the day before the accident and won't be back for a few weeks."

"You do know there's a way for you to find out the identity of your uninvited visitor, don't you?" Zane asked.

Derringer glanced over at him. "How?"

"Did you forget about the video cameras we had installed on your property to protect the horses, the week before your fall? Anyone pulling into your yard would be captured on film if they got as far as your front porch."

Derringer blinked when he remembered the video camera and wondered why he hadn't recalled it sooner. He got up from Zane's table and swiftly strode to the door. "I need to get home and check out that tape," he said without looking back.

"What happens when you find out who she is?" Zane called out.

He slowed to a stop and glanced over his shoulder. "Whoever she is, she will be sorry." He then turned and continued walking.

He meant what he said. Thanks to Zane, the mystery might have been solved. But once Derringer discovered the woman's identity, her nightmare for what she'd done would just be beginning, he thought, getting into his truck and driving away. He had a feeling *his* nightmare would continue until he found her—their night together had been so good, it haunted his dreams.

He made it back to Derringer's Dungeon in record time, and once inside his house he immediately went to his office to log on to his computer. The technician who had installed the video camera had told him he had access to the film from any computer anywhere with his IP address. This would be the first time he had reason to view the footage since the cameras had been installed.

A year ago his Westmoreland cousins from Montana had expanded their very successful horse-breeding and training business and had invited him, Jason and Zane to join as partners. Since all three were fine horsemen—although you couldn't prove how good he was, considering what had happened on Monday—they had jumped at the chance to be included. In anticipation of the horses that would be arriving, they had decided to install cameras on all three of their properties to make sure horse thieves, which were known to pop up every so often in these parts, didn't get any ideas about stealing from a Westmoreland.

Derringer hauled in a deep breath when the computer came to life and he typed in the code to get him to the video-camera channel and almost held his breath as he searched for the date he wanted. He then sat there, with his gaze glued to the computer screen, and waited with bated breath for something to show up.

It seemed it took forever before the lights of a vehicle came into view. The time indicated it wasn't early afternoon, not quite dark, but there had been a thunderstorm brewing. He then recalled it had been raining something awful with thunder and lightning flashing all around. At one point the intensity of it had awakened him.

He squinted at the image, trying to make out the truck that turned into his yard in the torrential rain. It seemed the weather worsened and rain started to pour down on the earth the moment the vehicle pulled into his yard.

It took only a second to recall whose SUV was in focus and he could only lean back in his chair, not believing what he was seeing. The woman who got out of her truck, battling the weather before tackling the huge box on his porch by dragging it inside his place was none other than Lucia Conyers.

He shook his head trying to make heads or tails of what he was seeing. Okay, he had it now. He figured, for whatever reason, Lucia had come by—probably as a favor to Chloe—to check on him and had been kind enough to bring the box inside the house, out of the rain.

He sat there watching the computer screen, expecting her to come back out at any minute and then get in her truck and pull off. He figured once she left, another vehicle would drive up, and the occupant of that car would be the woman he'd slept with. But as he sat there for another twenty minutes or so viewing the screen, Lucia never came back out.

Lucia Conyers was his Puddin' Tame?

Derringer shook his head, thinking that there was no way. He then decided to fast-forward the tape to five o'clock the next morning. His eyes narrowed suspiciously when a few minutes later he watched his front door open and Lucia ease out of it as if she was sneaking away from the scene of some crime. And she was wearing the same clothes she had on when she'd first arrived the night before. It was obvious she had dressed hurriedly and was moving rather quickly toward her SUV.

Damn. He couldn't believe it. He wouldn't believe it if he wasn't seeing it for himself. She was the one woman he would never have suspected, not in a million years. But from the evidence he'd gotten off his video camera, Lucia was the woman he had slept with. Lucia, his sister-in-law's best friend. Lucia was innocent—at least his assumption of that had been right. His mystery lover had been Lucia, the woman who would shy away from him and act skittish whenever he came around her.

Last month he recalled hearing Chloe and his sisters tease her about this being the last year of her twenties and challenge her to write a list of everything she wanted to do before hitting the big three-oh. He couldn't help wondering if she had added something outlandish like getting pregnant before her biological clock stopped ticking or ridding herself of her virginity.

Anger filled him, seeped through every pore in his body. Lucia Conyers had a hell of a lot of explaining to do. She better have a good reason for getting into bed with him that night two weeks ago.

He pulled his cell phone out of his pocket and punched in the number to his sister-in-law's magazine.

"*Simply Irresistible,* may I help you?"

"Yes, I'd like to speak to Lucia Conyers, please," he said, trying to control his anger.

"Sorry, but Ms. Conyers just stepped out for lunch."

"Did she say where she was going?" he asked.

The receptionist paused and then asked. "Who may I ask is calling?"

"This is Mr. Westmoreland."

"Oh, Mr. Westmoreland, how are you? Your wife and baby were here a couple of days ago, and your daughter looks just like you."

Derringer shook his head. Evidently the woman thought he was Ramsey, which was okay with him if he could get the information he wanted out of her.

"I take that as a compliment. Did Lucia say where she was going for lunch?"

"Yes, sir. She's dining at McKay's today."

"Thanks."

"You're welcome, sir."

Derringer hung up the phone and leaned back in his chair as an idea formed in his mind. He wouldn't let her know he had found out the truth about her visit. He would let her assume that she had gotten away with it and that he didn't have a clue that she was the woman who'd taken advantage of him that night.

And then when she least expected it, he would play his hand.

Three

Something, Lucia wasn't sure exactly what, made her glance over her menu and look straight into the eyes of Derringer Westmoreland. She went completely still as he moved in fluid precision toward her, with an unreadable expression on his face.

Staring at him, taking him all in, all six-three of him, while broad shoulders flexed beneath a blue Western shirt, and a pair of jeans clung to him like a second layer of skin and showed the iron muscles in his thighs. And then there was his face, too handsome for words, with his medium-brown skin tone, dark coffee-colored eyes and firm and luscious-looking lips.

For the moment she couldn't move; she was transfixed. A part of her wanted to get up quickly and run in another direction, but she felt glued to the chair. But that didn't stop liquid heat from pooling between her thighs when her gaze locked onto his face and she looked at the same features she had seen almost two weeks ago in his bed.

Why was he here and approaching her table? Had he found her panties and figured out she was the woman who had left them behind? She swallowed, thinking there was no way he could have discovered her identity, but then she asked herself why else would he seek her out?

He finally came to a stop at her table and she nervously moistened her lips with the tip of her tongue. She could swear his gaze was following her every movement. She swallowed again, thinking she had to be imagining things, and opened her mouth to speak. "Derringer? What are you doing here? Chloe mentioned you had taken a nasty fall a couple of weeks ago."

"Yes, but a man has to eat sometime. I was told McKay's serves the best potpie on Thursdays for lunch and there's always a huge crowd. I saw you sitting over here alone and thought the least we can do is help the place out," he said.

She was trying hard to follow him and not focus on the way his Adam's apple moved with every word he said, as if it was on some sensuous beat. She lifted a brow. "Help the place out in what way?"

He gave her a smooth smile. "Freeing up a table by us sharing one."

Lucia was trying really hard not to show any emotion—especially utter astonishment and disbelief—as well as not to let the menu she was holding fall to the floor. Had he just suggested that they share a table during lunch? Breathe the same air?

She was tempted to pick up the glass filled with ice water and drink the whole thing in one gulp. Instead, she drew in a deep breath to stop her heart from pounding so hard in her chest. How could spending only one night in his bed cause her to want to let go of her sensibilities and play out these newfound urges at the sight of him?

Of course, there was no way she would do something like that. In fact, a part of her was shaking inside at the thought he wanted to join her for lunch. She quickly wondered how Chloe would handle the situation if she was in her place. The answer came easy, but then she wasn't Chloe. However, she had to keep her cool and respond with the confidence Chloe possessed. The confidence that she lacked.

Lucia forced a smile to her lips. "I think that's a good idea, Derringer."

His lips eased into a smile right before her eyes. "Glad you agree," he said, taking the chair across from her.

She forced herself to breathe and belatedly realized just what she'd done. She had agreed to let him sit at her table. What on earth would they have to talk about? What if she let something slip and said something really stupid like, *"Oh, by the way, when can I drop by and get the panties I left behind the other night?"*

She sighed heavily. For all she knew, he might have figured things out already. Seriously, why else would he give a royal flip whether or not McKay's was crowded for lunch? That in itself was suspect because he'd never sought out her attention before.

She glanced over at him and he smiled at her, flashing those same dimples that he'd flashed that night she almost melted in her chair. He looked the same, only thing was that his eyes no longer had a hungover look. Today his gaze was as clear as glass.

The waitress saved them from talking when she walked up to take both their lunch orders. When she left, Lucia wished she had a mirror to see how she looked. She would die if she didn't at least look halfway decent. Absently, she ran a finger through her hair and pressed her lips together. She was grateful to feel her lipstick still in place, although she was tempted to get the tube of lipstick from her purse and apply a fresh coat.

"I understand you're back in school."

She was watching his mouth and his lips moved. She realized he'd said something. "Excuse me?"

He smiled again. "I said I heard you were back in school."

"Yes, I am. How did you know?"

"Chloe mentioned it."

"Oh." She wondered why Chloe would mention such a thing unless he'd asked about her. Had he? She shook her head, finding the idea unlikely. Her name must have popped up for conversational purposes and nothing more than that. If there had been anything more, Chloe definitely would have told her.

"Yes, I'm back at school taking night classes to get my master's degree in mass communications." Then, without missing a beat, she said, "You seem to be doing well from your fall." No sooner had the words left her mouth than she wished she could take them back.

Why on earth would she bring up anything relating to that day?

"Yes, but I'm doing better now. I've been taking it easy for the past week or so and sleeping most of the time. It helped. I feel in pretty good shape now."

She didn't know how to tell him that as far as she was concerned, he'd been in pretty good shape that night as well. His movements hadn't been hindered in any way. The thought of all he'd done to her sent heat soaring all through her body.

"So, what else have you been up to lately?"

Lucia felt her heart give a loud thump in her chest and wondered if he'd heard it. Dragging her gaze from her silverware, she thought that she could remember in vivid detail just what she'd been up to lately with him. Sitting across from her was the man who'd taken her virginity. The man who'd introduced her to the kind of pleasure she'd only read about in romance novels, and the man whom she'd loved forever. And knowing he probably had no idea of any of those things was the epitome of insane. But somehow she would fake it and come off looking like the most poised person that ever existed.

"Not a whole lot," she heard herself saying. "School and the magazine keep me pretty busy, but because I enjoy doing both I won't complain. What about you?" His gaze seemed to linger on her lips.

He chuckled. "Other than making a fool of myself with Sugar Foot, I haven't been up to a whole lot either."

She inclined her head. "What on earth would entice

you to ride that horse? I think everyone has heard how mean he is."

He chuckled and the sound was a low, sexy rumble that made goose bumps form on her arms. "Ego. I figured if Casey could do it then so could I."

She knew his cousin Casey and her husband, along with his cousin Durango and his wife, Savannah, had come visiting a few weekends ago. She'd heard everyone had been amazed at the ease with which Casey had gotten on Sugar Foot's back and held on even when the horse had been determined to get her off.

"I'm a pretty good horseman," Derringer said, breaking into her thoughts. "Although I'd be the first to admit I wasn't personally trained by the renowned and legendary Sid Roberts like Casey and her brothers while growing up."

Lucia nodded. His cousins Casey, Cole and Clint were triplets, and she had heard that they had lived with Roberts, their maternal uncle, while growing up. "We can all learn from the mistakes we make," she said, taking a sip of her water to cool off.

"Yes, we sure can."

Deciding she needed to escape, if only for a short moment, Lucia stood. "Would you excuse me for a moment? I need to go to the ladies' room."

"Sure, no problem," he said, standing.

Lucia drew in a deep breath, wishing she was walking out the restaurant door with no intention of returning and not just escaping to the ladies' room. And as she continued walking, she could actually feel Derringer staring at her back.

* * *

Derringer watched Lucia leave, thinking she looked downright sexy in her below-the-knee skirt and light blue pullover sweater. And then he couldn't help but admire her small waistline and the flare of her hips in the skirt as she walked. Standing about five-seven, she had a pair of nice-looking black leather boots on her feet, but he could recall just what a nice pair of legs she had and remembered how those legs had felt wrapped around him the night they'd made love.

He would be the first to admit that he'd always thought Lucia was pretty, with her smooth brown skin and lustrous shoulder-length black hair that she usually wore pulled back in a ponytail. Then there were her hazel eyes, high cheekbones, cute chin and slim nose. And he couldn't forget her luscious-looking mouth, one that could probably do a lot of wicked things to a man.

He leaned back in his chair remembering how years ago when she'd been about eighteen—about to leave home for college—and he had been in the process of moving back home from university, she had caught his eye. In memory of his parents and his aunt and uncle, who'd died together in a plane crash while he was in high school, the Westmorelands held a charity ball every year to raise money for the Westmoreland Foundation, which had been founded to aid various community causes. Lucia had attended the ball that year with her parents.

He had been standing by the punch bowl when she had arrived, and the sight of her in the dress she'd been wearing that night had rendered him breathless. He hadn't been able to take his eyes off her all evening. Evidently others had noticed his interest, and one of those had been her father, Dusty Conyers.

Later that same night the older man had pulled him aside and warned him away from his daughter. He let Derringer know in no uncertain terms that he would not tolerate a Westmoreland sniffing behind his daughter, creating the kind of trouble that Carl Newsome was having with Derringer's cousin Bane.

Bane had had the hots for Crystal Newsome since junior high school, and since Bane had a penchant for getting into trouble, Newsome hadn't wanted him anywhere near his daughter. Unfortunately, Crystal had other ideas and had been just as hot for Bane as he'd been for her, and Crystal and Bane managed to get into all kinds of naughty trouble together. Once, they'd even tried their hand at eloping before Carl Newsome had found his daughter and shipped her off to heaven knows where. A brokenhearted Bane had decided to take charge of his life by going into the Navy.

Derringer knew that although he didn't have Bane's badass reputation, he was still a Westmoreland, and a lot of mamas and daddies were dead set on protecting their daughters from what they thought was a Westmoreland heartbreak just waiting to happen. A part of him couldn't fault Dusty Conyers for being one of them; especially since Derringer had made it known far and wide that he had no plans to settle down with any one woman. A wife was the last thing on his mind then as well as now. Making a success of the horse-training business he'd just started was his top priority.

"I'm back."

He glanced up and stood for her to sit and thought that Lucia was even more beautiful up close. She had a nervous habit of licking her lips with her tongue. He would do just about anything to replace her tongue with his the next time she did it. And he also liked the sound of her voice. She spoke in a quiet yet sexy tone that did things to his insides, and he decided to keep her talking every chance he got.

"Tell me about the classes you're taking at the university and why you decided to go back and get your master's degree."

She lifted a brow and then her lips curved into one of her smiles again. Evidently, he'd hit on a subject she liked talking about. "Although Chloe hasn't made any announcements about anything, I can see her spending less and less time with *Simply Irresistible*. Whenever she does come into the office she has the baby with her, and it's obvious that she prefers being home with Susan and Ramsey."

He nodded, thinking he'd had that same impression as well. Whenever he paid Ramsey and Chloe a visit, they appeared to be a content and very happy couple who thoroughly enjoyed being parents. He'd heard from his other brothers that already Ramsey and Chloe were thinking about having another child.

"And I want to be prepared if she decides to take a leave of absence for a while," Lucia continued. "She and I talked about it, and because my bachelor's degree was in business, we thought it would be a good idea for me to get a degree in communications as well."

The waitress chose that moment to return with their

food, and once the plates had been placed in front of them, she left.

"I understand Gemma is adjusting to life in Australia."

He couldn't help but smile. Although he missed his sister, it seemed from all the phone calls they got that she *was* adjusting to life in Australia. He'd known Callum, the man who used to be the manager of Ramsey's sheep farm, had loved Gemma for a while, even if his sister had been clueless. He'd always known Callum's feelings for Gemma had been the real thing and not for the sole purpose of getting her into bed. He'd wholeheartedly approved of Gemma and Callum's relationship.

"Yes, I talked to her a few days ago. She and Callum are planning to come home for the Westmoreland Charity Ball at the end of the month." He wondered if she planned to go and if so, if she already had a date.

"Are you dating anyone seriously?" he decided to ask and set his plan into motion.

She looked over at him after popping a strawberry into her luscious mouth, chewed on it a moment, and then she swallowed it before replying. "The only dates I have these days are with my schoolbooks."

"Um, what a pity, that doesn't sound like a lot of fun. How about a movie this weekend?"

She cocked a surprised eyebrow. "A movie?"

He could tell his suggestion had surprised her. "Yes, a movie. Evidently, you're not spending enough time having fun, and everyone needs to let loose now and then. There's a new Tyler Perry movie coming out this weekend that I want to see. Would you like to go with me?"

Lucia's heart began pounding in her chest as she quickly reached the conclusion that Derringer had to have figured out that she was the woman who'd brazenly shared his bed. What other reason could he have for asking her out? Why the sudden interest in her when he'd never shown any before?

Their eyes held for what seemed like several electrifying moments before she finally broke eye contact with him. But what if he *didn't* know, and asking her out was merely a coincidence? There was only one way to find out. She glanced back over at him and saw he was still staring at her with that unreadable expression of his. "Why do you want to take me out, Derringer?"

He gave her a smooth smile. "I told you. You're spending too much time studying and working and need to have a little fun."

She still wasn't buying it. "We've known each other for years. Yet you've never asked me out before. In fact, you've never shown any interest."

He chuckled. "It wasn't that I didn't want to show an interest, Lucia, but I love my life and all my body parts."

She raised a brow and paused with the fork halfway to her mouth. "What do you mean?"

He took a sip of his iced tea and then his mouth curved ruefully. "I was warned away from you early on and took the warning seriously."

She nearly dropped the fork from her hand and had

to tighten her grip to place it back down. "What do you mean you were warned away from me?" That was impossible. She'd never had a boyfriend jealous enough to do such a thing.

A grin flashed across his face. "Your dad knows how to scare a man off, trust me."

Her head began spinning at the same time her heart slammed hard against her rib cage. "My dad warned you away from me?"

He smiled. "Yes, and I took him seriously. It was the summer you were about to leave for college. You were eighteen and I was twenty-two and returning home from university. You attended the Westmoreland Charity Ball with your parents before you left. He saw me checking you out, probably thought my interest wasn't honorable, and pulled me aside and told me to keep my eyes to myself or else…"

Lucia swallowed. She knew her dad. His bark was worse than his bite, but most people didn't know that. "Or else what?"

"Or else my eyes, along with another body part I'd rather not mention, would get pulled from their sockets. The last thing he would put up with was a Westmoreland dating his daughter."

Lucia didn't know whether to laugh or cry. She could see her father making a threat like that because he was overprotective of her. But she doubted Derringer knew how much his words thrilled her. He had been checking her out when she was eighteen?

She nervously moistened her lips with the tip of her tongue and couldn't help noticing the movement of his gaze to her mouth. Her skin began burning at the thought that he had been attracted to her even when she hadn't had a clue. But still…

"Aw, come on, Derringer, that was more than ten years ago," she said in a teasing tone.

"Yes, but you probably don't recall a few years ago I dropped by the paint store to make a purchase and you were working behind the counter and waited on me."

Oh, she definitely remembered that day, and three years later hadn't been able to forget it. But of course she couldn't tell him that. "That was a long time ago, but I think I remember that day. You needed a can of paint thinner." She could probably tell him what brand it was and exactly how much he'd paid for it.

"Yes, well, I had planned to ask you out then, but Mr. Conyers gave me a look that reminded me of the conversation we'd had years before and that his opinion of me pursuing you hadn't changed."

She couldn't help but laugh and it felt good. He had actually wanted to talk to her then, too. "I can't believe you were afraid of Dad."

"Believe it, sweetheart. He can give you a look that lets you know he means business. And it didn't help that he and Bane had had a run-in a few years before when Bane swiped a can of paint on display in front of the store and used it to paint some not-so-nice graffiti all over the front of Mr. Milner's feed store and signed off by saying it was a present from your father."

Lucia wiped tears of laughter from her eyes. "I was away at college, but I heard about that. Mom wrote and told me all the details. You're right, Dad was upset and so was Mr. Milner. Your cousin Bane had a reputation for getting into all kinds of trouble. How are things going with him and the Navy?"

"He's doing fine at the Naval Academy. It's hard to believe he's been gone for almost two years already, but he has."

"And he hasn't been back since he left?"

Derringer shook his head sadly. "No, not even once. He refuses to come back knowing Crystal isn't here, and he's still angry that he doesn't know where she is. The Newsomes made sure of that before they moved away. We are hoping he'll eventually forget her and move on, but so far he hasn't."

In a way, she knew how Bane felt. She hadn't looked forward to returning to Denver either, knowing she was still harboring feelings for Derringer. It was hard running into him while he was dating other girls and wishing they were her. And now to find out they could have been her. Her father had no idea what he'd done and the sad thing was that she couldn't get mad at him. Bane hadn't been the only Westmoreland with a reputation that had made it hard on the other family members. Derringer's younger brothers—the twins, Adrian and Aidan—as well as his baby sister Bailey had been Bane's sidekicks and had gotten into just as much trouble.

Needless to say, it had gotten to the point everyone in town would get up in arms when they saw any Westmoreland headed their way. But she had heard her father say more than once lately that considering everything, he thought Dillon and Ramsey had done a pretty good job in raising their siblings and in keeping the family together, and that he actually admired them for it. She knew that several people in town did. All the Westmorelands were college-educated and in some sort of business for themselves or holding prestigious jobs. And together they were the wealthiest family in the county and the largest landowners. People no longer feared them, they highly respected them.

"Just look how things turned out, Derringer," she heard herself say. "The twins are at Harvard. Bailey will be finishing up her studies at the university here in a year, and Bane is in the hands of Uncle Sam. Ramsey mentioned that Bane wants to become a Navy SEAL. In that case, he has to learn discipline, among other things."

Derringer chuckled. "For Bane, even with Uncle Sam, that won't be easy to do." He picked up his glass to take a sip of his iced tea. "So do we have a date for Saturday night or what?"

A date with Derringer Westmoreland…

She couldn't stop herself from feeling all giddy inside. She almost trembled at the thought. But at the same time she knew she had to be realistic. He would take her out on Saturday night and probably some other girl on Sunday. He'd asked her out to the movies, not a trip to Vegas to get married.

She would take the date for what it was and not put too much stock in it. She hadn't been born yesterday and she knew Derringer's reputation around town. He dated a lot, but let it be known that he didn't like women who clung or got too possessive.

Still, she couldn't help but smile at the thought that he was attracted to her and had been since she was eighteen. Didn't that account for something? She decided that it did.

"Yes, I'd love to go to the movies with you Saturday night, Derringer."

Four

Derringer frowned the moment he pulled into his yard and saw his sister Bailey's car parked there. The last thing he needed was for her to drop by to play nursemaid again. Megan was bad enough, but his baby sister Bailey was worse. She had only been seven when their parents had gotten killed. Now at twenty-two, she attended college full-time, and when she didn't have her nose stuck in some book it was stuck in her five brothers' personal affairs. She liked making it her business to know anything and everything about their comings and goings. Now that Ramsey was married, she'd given him some slack, but she hadn't let up with him, Zane and the twins.

He wondered how long she'd been there waiting on him and figured she probably wouldn't like the fact that he hadn't been home and had driven into town.

Since she wasn't out on the porch, that meant she had let herself inside, which wouldn't be a hard thing to do since he never locked his doors. His sister flung open the door the moment his foot touched the step. The look on her face let him know he was in trouble. She was there when the doctor restricted him from doing almost anything, other than breathing and eating, for two weeks.

"Just where have you been, Derringer Westmoreland, in your condition?"

He walked past her to put his hat on the rack. "And what condition is that, Bailey?"

"You're injured."

"Yes, but I'm not dead."

He regretted the words the moment they left his mouth when he saw the expression that suddenly appeared on her face. He and his brothers knew the real reason Bailey was so overprotective of them was that she was afraid of losing them the way she'd lost their parents.

But he could admit to having the same fears, and if he were to analyze things further, he would probably conclude that Zane had them as well. All of them had been close to their parents, aunt and uncle. Everyone had taken their deaths hard. The way Derringer had managed to move on, and not look back, was by not getting too attached to anyone. He had his cousins and his siblings. He loved them, and they were all he needed. If he were to fall in love, give his heart to a woman, and then something were to happen to her—there was no telling how he'd handle it, or even if he could. He liked things just the way they were. And, for that reason, he doubted he would ever marry.

He crossed the room and placed a hand on her shoulder when he saw her trembling. "Hey, come on, Bail, it wasn't that bad. You were there at the hospital and heard what Dr. Epps said. It's been almost two weeks now and I'm fine."

"But I also heard him say that it could have been worse, Derringer."

"But it wasn't. Look, unless you came to cook for me or do my laundry, you can visit some other time. I'm going to take a nap."

He saw the sad look on her face turn mutinous and knew his ploy had worked. She didn't like it when he bossed her around or came across as if she was at his beck and call. "Cook your own damn meals and do your own laundry, or get one of those silly girls who fawn all over you to do it."

"Whatever. And watch your mouth, Bailey, or I'll think you're slipping back to your old ways and I'll have to wash your mouth out with soap."

She grabbed the remote off the table, dropped down on the sofa and began watching television, ignoring him. He glanced at his watch and fought to hide his smile. "So, how long are you staying?" he asked. Because she hadn't yet inherited her one hundred acres, she had a tendency to spend time at any of their places. Most of the time she stayed with Megan, which suited all her brothers just fine because Bailey had a tendency to drop in unannounced at the most inconvenient times.

Like now.

She didn't even look over at him when she finally

answered his question. "I'm staying until I'm ready to leave. You have a problem with it?"

"No."

"Good," she said, using the remote to flip to another channel. "Now go take your nap and I hope when you wake up you're in a lot better mood."

He chuckled as he leaned down and planted a brotherly kiss on her forehead. "Thanks for worrying about me so much, kid," he said softly.

"If me, Megan and Gemma don't do it, who will? All those silly girls you mess around with are only after your money."

He lifted a brow in mock surprise. "You think so?"

She glanced up at him and rolled her eyes. "If you don't know the truth about them then you're in real trouble, Derringer."

Derringer chuckled again thinking yes, he knew the truth about them…especially one in particular. Lucia Conyers. He didn't think of her as one of those "silly girls" and knew Bailey wouldn't either. He would be taking Lucia to the movies Saturday night. He intended to return her panties to her then. He looked forward to the moment her mouth fell open and she realized he knew what she'd done and had known all this time. He couldn't wait to see what excuse she would come up with for what she had done.

Before heading up the stairs, he decided to feel his sister out about something. "I ran into Lucia Conyers a few moments ago at McKay's."

Bailey didn't take her gaze off the television and for a moment he thought that possibly she hadn't heard him, but then she responded. "And?"

He smiled. "And we shared a table since McKay's was crowded." He paused a moment. "She's pretty. I never realized just how pretty she is." The latter he knew wasn't true, because he'd always known how pretty she was.

He watched as Bailey slowly turned toward him with a frown on her face. "I hope you're not thinking what I think you're thinking."

He smiled. "Oh, I don't know. What do you think I'm thinking?"

"That you plan to hit on Lucia."

He grinned. "If by 'hit on her' you mean ask her out, I've already done so. We have a date to go to the movies this Saturday night."

Bailey's eyes widened. "Are you crazy? That's Chloe's best friend."

Now it was his turn. "And?"

"And everybody around these parts knows how most of the single male Westmorelands operate. You're used to those silly girls and wouldn't know how to appreciate a woman with sense like Lucia."

"You don't think so?"

"I know so and if you end up doing something stupid like hurting her, Chloe would never forgive you for it."

He shrugged at the thought. Chances were, Chloe had no idea what her best friend had pulled that night. And as far as what Bailey said about Lucia's having sense, he didn't doubt that, which made him uneasy about just what she would gain from tumbling into bed with him.

"Lucia is an adult. She can handle me," he said.

He wouldn't break it down and tell her that Lucia *had* handled him and had done a real good job doing so. He got a hard-on every time he thought about that night.

"I'm still warning you, Derringer. And besides being Chloe's best friend, Megan, Gemma and I like her as well."

He cocked an amused brow. "I guess that means a lot. The three of you never like any of the girls I date. I'll have to keep that in mind."

Without giving his kid sister time to say anything else, he quickly moved up the stairs for his nap.

Lucia couldn't wait to get back to her office to give Chloe a call and tell her about her date on Saturday night with Derringer.

"I'm happy for you," Chloe said with a smile in her voice that Lucia heard. "Falling off that horse must have knocked some sense into him. At least you know why he never approached you before. I can see your dad warning him off. I heard the Westmorelands had quite a reputation back in the day."

Lucia nodded. "And you think I did the right thing in agreeing to go out with him?"

"Come on, Lucia, don't you dare ask me that. You've loved the guy forever. You've even gone so far as to sleep with him."

She drew in a deep, ragged breath. "But he doesn't know that. At least I don't think he does."

"You honestly think he doesn't know?"

"I assumed he did and that was the only reason he wanted to share my table."

She heard Chloe bristle at that assumption. "Why

do you continue to think you're no match for Derringer when you're classier than all those other women he messes around with?"

"But that's just it, Chloe. I'm not the kind of woman he prefers, the kind he has a history of dating. I can't hold a candle to someone like Ashira Lattimore. And everyone knows she has been vying for his attention for years."

"I've met her and she's spoiled, self-centered, possessive and clingy. Definitely not wife material."

"Wife material?" Lucia laughed. "A wife is the furthest thing from Derringer's mind. You know that as well as I do."

"Yes, but I'm sure a lot of people said the same thing about Ramsey before I arrived on the scene. So that means a man's mind can change with the right woman. All you have to do is convince Derringer you're the right woman."

Lucia cringed at the thought of trying to do that. She wouldn't even know where to begin. "That's easy for you to say and do, Chloe. You've always been sure of yourself in everything you did."

"In that case, maybe you ought to try it for yourself. Just think, Lucia. Evidently Derringer is on your hook and now you have the chance to reel him right on in. You know how I feel about missed opportunities. How would things have turned out had I accepted Ramsey's refusal to be on the cover of my magazine? I saw what I wanted and decided to go after it. I think you should use that same approach."

"I don't know," Lucia said on a heavy sigh. This wasn't the first time Chloe had made that suggestion.

A part of her knew her friend was right, but what she was suggesting was easier said than done. At least for her it was.

"Think about it. Saturday is only two days away and if I were you, when Derringer arrived at my place to pick me up I'd make sure he would take one look at me and know he would enjoy every minute of his time in my presence. Now's your chance, Lucia. Don't let it go by without taking advantage of it."

A few moments later, after hanging up the phone with Chloe, indecisiveness weighed heavy in her chest. More than anything she would love to pique Derringer's interest, but what if she failed in her efforts to do so? What if she couldn't get the one man she loved to want to love her back? Was there a possibility that she was wrong about the type of women Derringer actually preferred?

One thing Chloe had said was true. No one would have figured that Ramsey Westmoreland would have fallen for any woman. The man had been set in his ways for years and the last woman he'd attempted to marry had announced she was pregnant from another man in the middle of the wedding. Yet, he had fallen in love with Chloe, whether he had wanted to or not. So maybe there was hope for all those other single Westmorelands; but especially for Derringer.

"I've heard you're interested in women's under-garments these days, Derringer. Is there a reason why?"

Derringer slowly turned away from the pool table with a cue stick in his hand to gaze at each man in the dimly lit room inside his basement. Now that he knew who his late-night visitor had been, he wouldn't tell anyone, not even Zane, her identity.

"No reason," he answered his cousin Canyon who was four years younger.

Canyon smiled. "Well, you never got around to asking me anything, but just so you know, the women I date don't wear underwear."

Derringer shook his head and chuckled. He didn't find that hard to believe. He studied the other men who had gone back to sipping their beers while waiting their turn at shooting pool—his brother Zane and his cousins Jason, Riley, Canyon and Stern. They were as close as brothers. Zane knew more than the others about the situation with him and the underwear, but Derringer was confident his brother wouldn't say anything.

"So, what's this I hear about you going on a date with Lucia? I thought old man Conyers pretty much scared you off her years ago," Jason said, chuckling.

Derringer couldn't help but smile. "He did, but like you said, it was years ago. Lucia isn't a kid anymore. She's an adult and old enough to make her own decisions about who she wants to date."

"True, but she's not your type and you know it," Riley piped in.

Derringer lifted a brow. That was the same thing Bailey had alluded to earlier that day. "And what, sup-posedly, is my type?"

"Women who wear black panties," Canyon said, chuckling.

"Or no panties at all," Riley added, laughing.

"Hmm, for all you all know, my taste in women

might have changed," he said, turning back to the pool table.

Zane snorted. "Since when? Since you got thrown off Sugar Foot's back and hit your head?"

Derringer frowned as he turned back around. "I didn't hit my head."

"Makes us wonder," Riley said. "First you're going around asking about women's underwear and now you're taking Lucia Conyers out on a date. You better treat her right or Chloe will come gunning for you."

"Hell, we'll all come gunning for you," Zane said, taking a sip of his beer. "We like her."

Derringer turned back to the pool table and proceeded to chalk his stick. At the moment, he didn't give a royal flip how his family felt about Lucia. He still planned to deal with her in his own way and if they didn't like the outcome that was too bad.

Five

By the time seven o'clock came around on Saturday night, Lucia was almost a nervous wreck. She had pulled her father aside that week to verify what Derringer had told her. With a sheepish grin on his face, Dusty Conyers hadn't denied a thing, and had laughingly agreed he had intentionally put the fear of God in Derringer. He didn't regret doing so and was glad it had worked.

He did agree that now she was old enough to handle her own business and wouldn't butt in again. She had ended up giving him a kiss on his bald head after telling him how much she loved him, and that he was the best dad in the whole wide world.

His confirmation meant that what Derringer had said the other day was true. He had shown interest in her years ago, but her father had discouraged him. Although she knew she would always wonder how things might have gone if her father hadn't intervened, she was a firm believer that things happened for a reason. Besides, at eighteen she doubted she would have been able to handle the likes of Derringer Westmoreland and was even doubtful she could have at twenty-two. She wasn't even confident she had the ability to handle him now, but was determined to try. She was convinced there was a reason she had shared his bed that night.

She just wished she had a clue what that reason was.

She was grateful that one didn't have anything to do with the other. The reason he had asked her out had nothing to do with them sleeping together and she felt good about that. She had played the details of their night together over and over in her mind so many times that she knew practically every single movement by heart.

All week she had found herself going to bed but unable to sleep until she replayed in her mind every sensation she'd felt that night. It didn't take much to remember how it felt to grip his iron-steel shoulders beneath her fingers while he thrust in and out of her. The thought of making love with a man like Derringer sent sensuous chills up her spine.

She knew the exact moment Derringer pulled into her driveway. From the smooth hum of the engine she could tell he was driving his two-seater sports car instead of his truck. That meant the car's interior would be that much cozier. The thought of being in such proximity to Derringer stirred all kinds of feelings inside.

She had spoken to Chloe earlier and her best friend had said the Westmorelands were torn as to whether or not her dating Derringer was a good idea, considering his history with women. Bottom line was that no one wanted to see her get hurt. But what they didn't know was that she had loved Derringer so long that to her tonight was really a dream come true. And if he never asked her out again that would be fine because she would always have memories of tonight to add to those she had of that Monday night. Not that she expected things would get as heated tonight as they had in his bedroom, mind you. But she couldn't wait to see what was in store for her tonight. Just knowing she was Derringer's date made her feel good inside, and knowing he had no ulterior motive in taking her out made it that much more special.

Derringer smiled when he pulled into Lucia's driveway, thinking her house was the brightest on the block with floodlights in every corner, the porch light on and a light pole shining in the front of the yard. He thought it was a real nice neighborhood with beautiful trees on both sides of the street and the silhouette of mountains in the background. But he felt crowded. One of the pitfalls of being a Westmoreland was that because each of them owned a hundred acres of land, living anywhere else would seem restrictive and too confining.

As he walked up to the porch, he felt as if he was under the bright lights and wouldn't be surprised if some of her neighbors were watching him. In fact, he was certain he saw the front curtain move in the house across the street. He chuckled, thinking if she could deal with her nosy neighbors then he certainly could.

Besides, he had enough on his plate dealing with his own nosy relatives. Maybe it had been a bad idea to mention his date to Bailey. She hadn't wasted time spreading the word. He'd gotten a number of calls warning him he had best behave tonight—whatever that meant. And yet, the one call he'd expected, the one from Chloe, had never come. That made him wonder if she knew a lot more than he thought she did.

He glanced at his watch before ringing Lucia's doorbell. It was seven-thirty exactly. He'd made good time and since he'd already reserved tickets online, they wouldn't have to stand in line at the theater. He had thought of everything, including when would be the best time to drop the bomb on her about that night. He had decided that they would enjoy the movie first before dealing with any unpleasantness.

He heard the lock turn on her door and then seconds later she was standing there, illuminated in the doorway. He blinked in surprise when he gazed down at her. She looked different. She'd always been a pretty girl, but tonight she looked absolutely stunning.

Gone was the ponytail. Instead, her hair was curled and fell in feathered waves to her shoulders. And she had done something with her eyes that made them look more striking and the entire look somehow showcased her dazzling sophistication.

And then there was the outfit she was wearing. Not too daring, but enough to keep him on the edge all evening. Her sweater dress was a plum color and she had black suede boots on her feet. She wasn't overly dressed for the movie and he thought her attire was perfect... and it fit her just that way, emphasizing her small waist, and falling above the knees, it definitely showed off a beautiful pair of thighs encased in tights.

A second passed and then several before he was able to open his mouth to speak, and from the smile that touched her lips she was well aware of the effect she was having on him. He couldn't help but smile back. She had definitely pulled one over on him. Gone was just the "pretty" Lucia and in her place stood a creature so gorgeous that she took his breath away.

"Derringer."

He exhaled an even breath. At least he tried to. "Lucia."

"I just need to get my jacket. Would you like to come in for a second?" she asked.

He felt another smile pull at his lips. She was inviting him in. "Sure."

When he brushed by her, he almost buckled to his knees when he took a whiff of her perfume. It was the same scent he had awakened to that Tuesday morning. The same scent that was all in his head. She was the one woman who had him sleeping each night with her panties under his pillow. He took in a deep breath to pull more of the fragrance into his nostrils. There was just something potent about the scent of a woman.

"Would you like a drink before we leave?"

"No, but thanks for the offer," he said, glancing around her living room.

"It won't take but a minute to grab my jacket."

"Take your time," he said, watching as she walked away, appreciating her movements in the dress, especially how it fit her from behind. He forced his gaze away from her when she entered her bedroom and continued his study of her house, thinking it was small but just the right size for her. And it was tidy, not a single thing out of place, even the magazines on the table seemed to lie in a perfect position. He liked her fireplace and could imagine how it would look with a fire blazing in it. He could imagine her on the floor, stretched out in front of it on one of those days that was cold, snowy and dreary outside.

On the drive over, he did notice that this particular subdivision was centrally located to just about everything; shopping, fast-food places, grocery stores and a dry cleaner. That had to be pretty advantageous to her. He rolled his eyes wondering why the heck he cared if it was or not.

"I'm ready now, Derringer."

He turned and glanced back at her. She was standing beside a floor lamp and the lighting totally captured her beauty. For a moment he just stood there and stared, unable to tear his gaze away from her. What the hell was wrong with him? He knew the answer when he felt blood rush straight to his groin. It would be so easy for him to suggest that they forget about the movie and hang here instead. But he knew he couldn't do that.

However, there was something he could do, something he definitely felt compelled to do at that moment. He slowly moved toward her with his heart pounding hard in his chest with every step he took. And when he stood directly in front of her, he said the only words he could say at that moment. Words he knew were totally true. "You look simply beautiful tonight, Lucia."

Lucia didn't know what to say. His compliment caused soothing warmth to spread all through her. In the back of her mind something warned her that the man was smooth, sophisticated and experienced. Like most men, he would say just about anything to score. But at that moment she didn't care. The compliment had come from Derringer Westmoreland and to her that meant everything.

"Thank you, Derringer."

He lowered his head a little, bent low to murmur in her ear, "You're so very welcome."

He kept his head lowered to that angle and she knew without a shadow of a doubt that he intended to kiss her. And that knowledge caused several heated anticipatory sensations to flow from the toes of her feet to the crown of her head.

"Lucia?"

The throaty tone of his voice seemed to stroke everything within her and was doing so effortlessly.

"Yes?"

He lifted his hand to cradle her chin and tilt her face up to his. Her pulse rate increased when a slow smile touched his lips the moment their eyes connected. "I need to kiss you." And before she could draw her next breath, he lowered his mouth to hers.

He had kissed her that night numerous times in the throes of passion, but she immediately thought this kiss was different. The passion was still there, but unlike before it wasn't flaming out of control. What he was doing was slowly and deliberately robbing her senses of any and all control.

His tongue eased between her lips on a breathless moan and he seemed in no hurry to do anything but stand there, feed on every angle of her mouth, every nook and cranny. His kiss burned her in its wake, sharing its heat. He tasted like the peppermint candy he'd obviously been sucking on earlier.

But now he was sucking on her—her tongue at least; and he wasn't letting up as he probed deeply, gently but thoroughly, plunging her into an oasis of sensations as his tongue continued to sweep over her mouth.

She felt something roll around in her belly at the same time he moved his body closer, and automatically the cradle of her thighs nestled the hard erection pressing against her, causing an ache that was so engaging she couldn't do anything but moan.

This was the sort of kiss most men left a girl with after a date and not before the start of their evening. But evidently no one told that to Derringer and he was showing her there was no particular order in the way he did things. He made his own rules, set his own parameters. Now she knew why he was so high in demand with women, and why fathers warned him not to pursue their daughters. And why heat could resonate off his body like nobody's business.

But tonight he was making it her *business.*

He shifted the intensity of the kiss without warning and the hands that were already wrapped around her waist tightened in a possessive grip. The probing of his tongue deepened and she could only stand there and continue to moan while her pulse throbbed erratically in her throat. Her hips moved instinctively against his and the heat that spread lower all through her belly didn't slow down any.

There was no telling how long they would have stood there, going at each other's mouths, if she hadn't pulled back for air. She closed her eyes and took a deep breath, licking her lips and and tasting him on her tongue. The pleasure she felt just being kissed by him was almost unbearable. She slowly opened her eyes to calm the turbulent emotions inside her.

For the second time that night, his hand lifted to capture her chin, lifting her face to meet his gaze. The look in his eyes was dark, intense, sexually hungry. At that moment, he looked as rugged as the landscape in which he lived. Westmoreland country. She never realized until now just how much that had defined him. She continued to hold his gaze. Mesmerized. Falling deeper and deeper in love.

"You, Lucia Conyers, are more than I bargained for," he said in a deep, husky tone that sounded intimate and overwhelming at the same time.

She chuckled unevenly while wondering if this was how a kiss could easily get out of hand. Was this how a couple could take a kiss to another level without realizing they'd done so until it was too late to do anything about it?

"Is being more than you bargained for a good thing or a bad thing, Derringer?" she asked him.

He laughed softly at her question and released her chin, but not before lowering his head and brushing his lips across hers. "I'll let you decide that later," he whispered hotly against her lips. "Come on. Let's get out of here while we can."

Tonight was not going the way he'd planned, Derringer thought. Even the smell of popcorn couldn't get rid of her scent. His nostrils were inflamed with it. This was their first date and he had fully intended for it to be their last.

But...

And there was a *but* in there someplace. For him there were probably several and each of them were messing with his mind. Making him not want to end their evening together. Or to spoil just how good things were going between them.

After the movie he suggested they go to Torie's for coffee. She was everything a man could appreciate in a date, while at the same time not fully what a man expected—but in a positive way. She had the ability to ease into a conversation that wasn't just about her. And as he maneuvered his sports car through downtown Denver, he quickly reached the conclusion that he liked the sound of her voice and in the close confines of the car, her scent continued to overtake his senses.

Derringer couldn't help but wonder if there was something with this "scent of a woman" theory that men often talked about behind closed doors and in dimly lit, whiskey-laden poolrooms. Over his lifetime he had encountered a lot of women who smelled good, but the one sitting next to him right now, whose eyes were closed as she took in the sound of John Legend on his CD player, not only smelled good but was good to smell. And he decided then and there that there was a difference. He chuckled and shook his head at his conclusion.

"Um, what's so funny?" she asked, opening her eyes and turning her head to glance over at him.

"I was just thinking about the movie," he lied, knowing there was no way he would tell her what really had amused him.

She laughed lazily. "It was good, wasn't it?"

When the car slowed in traffic, he gave her a sidelong glance. "Yes, it was. Are you comfortable?"

"Yes. And thanks. This car is nice."

"Glad you like it." He was certain his smile flashed in the dimly lit interior. He appreciated any woman who liked his car. A number of his former dates had complained that although his car was sleek and fast, it was not roomy enough.

"Can you believe they are expecting snow next weekend?"

He chuckled. "Hey, this is Denver. Snowstorms are always expected." They passed a moment in silence. "Did you enjoy living in Florida those four years?"

She nodded. "Immensely."

"Then why did you return to Denver?"

She didn't answer right away. "Because I couldn't imagine living anywhere else," she said finally.

He nodded, understanding completely. Although he had enjoyed living in Phoenix while attending college, he never could wait to return home...to see her again. He hadn't been back a week when Ramsey had sent him into town to pick up a can of paint thinner and he'd seen her again.

At first he'd been taken aback, nearly not recognizing her. She had gone from the gangly young girl to a twentysomething-year-old woman who had grown into a beauty that he had noticed right away. It was a good thing her father had been on guard and had intervened again, because there was no telling where his lustful mind would have led him that day. She had gotten spared from being added to the list as one of Derringer's Pleasers. When he'd returned home it seemed women had come out of the woodwork vying for his attention.

They soon arrived at Torie's, an upscale coffee shop that was known for its signature award-winning coffee and desserts. He helped her out of his sports car, very much aware of the looks they were getting. But now, unlike the other times, he wasn't so sure the focus was on his specially-designed Danish car and not on the woman he was helping out of it. For the first time since he could remember, he relinquished the car to the valet without giving the young man a warning look and strict instructions to be careful on how his prize was handled.

"Mr. Westmoreland, it's nice to see you," the maître d' greeted when they entered the coffee shop.

"Thanks, Pierre. And I'd like a private table in the back."

"Most certainly."

He cupped Lucia's arm as they were led to a table that overlooked the mountains and a lake. The fire that was blazing in the fireplace added the finishing touch. A romantic setting that for even someone like him—a man who probably didn't have a romantic bone in his body until it suited him—was clearly defined. "We can have just coffee if you like, but their strawberry cheesecake is good," he said, smiling when they were seated.

Lucia chuckled. "I'm going to take your word for it and try some."

The waiter came to take their drink order. She ordered a glass of wine and when he ordered only a club soda she glanced over at him curiously. "I'm driving, remember? And I'm still on medication," he said by way of explanation. "And the doctor was adamant about me not consuming alcohol while I'm taking them."

She nodded. "Are you still in pain?"

A rueful smile touched his lips. "Not unless I move too fast. Otherwise, I'm doing fine."

"I guess you won't be getting on Sugar Foot's back again any time soon."

"What makes you say that? In fact, I plan to try him again tomorrow."

Her look of horror and disbelief was priceless, he thought, and he chuckled as he reached across the table to engulf her hand in his. "Hey, I was just kidding."

She frowned over at him. "I hope so, Derringer, and I certainly hope you've learned your lesson about taking unnecessary risks."

He laughed. "Trust me, I have," he said, although he knew she was a risk and he had a feeling spending too much time with her wasn't a good thing. It was then that he realized he was still holding her hand, and with supreme effort he released it.

He should know better than to get too attached to a woman like Lucia. She was the kind of woman a man could become attached to before he knew it. His attraction to her seemed too natural, but way too binding. She was a woman who seemed to be created just for the purpose of making a man want her in ways he had never wanted a woman before. And that wasn't good.

After their initial drinks, they ordered coffee and then shared a slice of strawberry cheesecake, and while they sat there she had his undivided attention. They conversed about a number of topics. More than once he caught his gaze roaming across her face, studying her features and appreciating her beauty. Whether she knew it or not, her facial bone structure was superb and any man would definitely find her attractive. But he knew there was more to her than just her outside beauty. She was beautiful on the inside as well. Derringer listened as she told him about a number of charities and worthwhile events she supported, and he was impressed.

A couple of hours later while driving her back home, he couldn't help but reflect on how the evening had gone. Certainly not the way he had planned. When the car came to a traffic light, he glanced over at her. Not surprisingly, she had fallen asleep. He thought about all the things he wanted to do to her when he got her back to her place, and knew the only thing he should do was walk her to her door and then leave. Something was going on with him that he didn't understand and he was smart enough to know when to back off.

That thought was still on his mind when he walked her to the door later. For some reason, he was being pulled in another direction and frankly he didn't like it. Her kiss alone had shot his brain cells to hell and back and knocked his carefully constructed plans to teach her a lesson to the wind. Even now the taste from her kiss was lingering in his mouth.

"Thanks again for such a wonderful evening, Derringer. I had a great time."

He'd had a great time, too. "You're welcome." He forced his lips closed to stop from asking her out again. He simply refused to do that. "Well, I guess I'll be going now," he said, trying to get his feet to step back and trying to figure out why they wouldn't budge.

"Would you like to come inside for more coffee?"

He shook his head. "Thanks, but I don't think my stomach can hold much more. Besides, my restrictions are over and I can return to work soon. I'll be helping Zane and Jason with the horses in the morning. I need to get home and get to bed."

"All right."

He made a move to leave but couldn't. Instead, his gaze settled on the face staring at him and he felt something pull at his gut. "Good night, Lucia," he whispered, just seconds before leaning down and brushing a kiss across her lips.

"Good night, Derringer."

He straightened and watched as she let herself inside the house. When the door clicked locked behind her, he turned to move down the walkway toward his car. He opened the door and slid inside. He needed to go home and think about things, regroup and revamp. And he had to figure out what there was about Lucia Conyers that got to him on a level he wasn't used to.

Six

Zane stopped saddling his horse long enough to glance over at his brother. "What's going on with you, Derringer? Last week you were inquiring about women's panties and now this week you want to know about a woman's scent. Didn't you get that mystery solved by viewing the tape on that video camera?"

Derringer rubbed his hand down his face. He should have known better than to come to Zane, but the bottom line was his brother knew more about women than *he* did and right now he needed answers. After he got them he'd be able to figure out what was going on with him when it came to Lucia. It had been almost a week after their date to the movies and he still didn't have a clue. And he had yet to confront her about being his late-night visitor.

He glanced over at Zane across the horse's back.

"There's nothing going on with me. Just answer the damn question."

Zane chuckled. "Getting kind of testy, aren't you? And how did your date go with Lucia Saturday night? I haven't heard you say."

"And I'm not going to say either, other than we had a nice time."

"For your sake I think that's all you better say or Chloe, Megan and Bailey will be coming down on you pretty hard. You might get a reprieve from Gemma since she's out of the country, but I wouldn't count on it if I were you, because she's coming home later this month for the charity ball."

Derringer grunted. The women in his family ought to stay out of his business and he would tell them so if the topic of Lucia ever came up with any of them again. So far, he'd been lying low this week, and when he had dropped by to see Ramsey, Chloe and baby Susan, the topic of Lucia hadn't come up. He could inwardly admit the reason he'd made himself scarce was his fear of running into her at Ramsey's. It was unheard of for Derringer Westmoreland to avoid any woman.

"So, will you answer my question?"

Zane crossed his arms over his chest. "Only after you answer mine. Did you or did you not watch that video footage?"

He glared over at his brother. "Yes, I watched it."

"And?"

"And I'd rather not discuss it."

A smirk appeared on Zane's face. "I bet you'll be glad to discuss it if you get hit with a paternity suit nine months from now."

Zane's words hit Derringer below the belt with a reminder that Lucia could be pregnant with his child. They'd had unprotected sex that night. She had to know that as well. Was she not worried about that possibility? He met his brother's intense gaze. "I'll handle it if that were to happen, now answer the question."

Zane smiled. "You're going to have to repeat it. My attention span isn't what it used to be these days."

Like hell it's not, Derringer thought. He knew Zane was trying to get a rise out of him and he didn't like it, but since he needed answers he would overlook his brother's bad attitude for now. "I want to know about the scent of a woman."

Zane smiled as he leaned back against the corral post. "Um, that's an easy one. Every woman has her own unique scent and if a man is attentive enough he's able to tell them apart by it. Some men will know their woman's location in a room before setting eyes on her just from her scent alone."

Derringer pulled in a deep breath. He knew all that already. He tilted his Stetson back off his head. "What I want to know is the effect that scent can have on a man."

Zane chuckled. "Well, I know for a fact that a woman's natural scent is a total turn-on for most men. It's all in the pheromones. Remember that doctor I dated last year?"

Derringer nodded. "Yes, what about her?"

"Man, her scent used to drive me crazy, and she damn well knew it. But it didn't bother me one bit when she took that job in Atlanta and moved away," Zane said.

Derringer decided not to remind Zane of the bad mood he'd been in for months after the woman left. "Every woman has her unique scent, but many douse it with cologne," Zane continued. "Then every woman that wears that cologne practically smells the same. But when you make love to a woman, her natural scent will override everything."

Zane paused a minute and then said, "And the effect it can have on a man depends on what degree of an attractant her scent can be. A woman's scent alone can render him powerless."

Derringer lifted his brow. "Powerless?"

"Yes, the scent of a woman is highly potent and sexually stimulating. And some men have discovered their own male senses can detect the woman who was meant to be their mate just from her scent. Animals rely on scent for that purpose all the time, and although some people might differ with that theory, there are some who believes it's true for humans as well. So if the scent of some woman is getting to you, that might be your cue she's your mate."

Derringer studied his brother's gaze, not sure if Zane was handing him a bunch of bull or not. The thought of his future being shared with a woman because of her scent didn't make much sense, but he'd watched enough shows on *Animal Kingdom* to know that was basically true with animals. Was man different from other animals?

"Some woman's scent has gotten to you," Zane taunted.

He didn't answer. Instead, he looked away for a second, wondering about that same thing. When he looked back at Zane moments later, his brother was grinning.

"What the hell do you find amusing?"

"Trust me, you don't want to know."

Derringer frowned. Zane was right; he didn't want to know.

"And you haven't heard from Derringer since your date Saturday night?"

A lump formed in Lucia's throat with Chloe's question. It was Friday night, late afternoon, and she sat curled on her sofa. Although she really hadn't expected Derringer to seek her out again, the notion that he didn't still bothered her, especially because she thought they'd had such a good time. At least she knew for a fact *she* had, and he'd seemed to enjoy himself as well. But she figured when you were Derringer Westmoreland, you could have a different girl every day.

When he had brought her home Saturday night, she had expected him to accept her invitation to come inside for coffee, although she would be the first to admit they had drunk plenty of the stuff at Torie's. He had declined her offer and given her a chaste kiss on the lips then left.

"No, I haven't heard anything, but that's okay. I was able to write in my diary that I had a date with him and that's good."

"One date isn't good when there can be others, Lu. You do know that women don't have to wait for the man to call for a date, we have that right as well."

Yes, but Lucia knew she couldn't be that forward with a man. "I know, but—"

There was a knock at her door. "Someone's at the door, Chloe. It's probably Mrs. Noel from across the street. She bakes on Fridays and uses me as her guinea pig, but I have no complaints. I'll call you back later."

When the knock sounded again, she called out after hanging up the phone. "I'm coming."

She eased off the sofa and headed to the door, thinking she would chow down on Mrs. Noel's sweets and get her romance groove on by watching a romantic movie on Lifetime. If you couldn't have the real thing in your life then she figured a movie was second best.

She nearly choked when she glanced out her peep-hole. Her caller wasn't her neighbor. It was Derringer. She suddenly felt hot when she realized he was staring at the peephole in the door as if he knew she was watching him. She closed her eyes trying to slow down the beating of her heart. He was the last person she expected to see tonight. In fact, she'd figured he wouldn't appear on her doorstep any time soon, or ever again. She assumed they would get back into the routine of running into each other whenever she visited Chloe, Ramsey and the baby.

Forcing her brain cells to stop scrambling, she turned the doorknob to open the door and there he stood in a pair of jeans, a sweater, a leather jacket and boots. He looked good, but then he always did. He was leaning against a post on her porch with his hands in his pockets.

She cleared her throat. "Derringer, what are you doing here?"

He held her gaze. "I know I should have called first."

She stopped herself from saying that he could appear on her doorstep anytime. The last thing a woman should do is let a man assume she was pining for him...even if she was. "Yes, you should have called first. Is anything wrong?"

"No, I just needed to see you."

She tried to ignore how low his voice had dropped and how he was looking at her. Instead, she tried to focus on what he'd said. *He just needed to see her.*

Yeah, right. She thought he could really do better than that, especially since he hadn't done so much as picked up a phone to call her since their date on Saturday night. Was she to believe needing to see her had brought him to her door? She wondered if his date tonight had canceled and she had been his backup plan. Curious about that possibility, she decided to ask him.

Crossing her arms over her chest, she said. "Um, let me guess, your date stood you up and I was next on the list." After saying the words, she realized her mistake. First, she doubted very seriously that any woman stood him up and she really thought a lot of herself to even assume she was on any list he had.

He tilted his head as if he needed to see her more clearly. "Is that what you think?"

She shook her head. "To be honest with you, Derringer, I really don't know what to think."

He made a slow move and inched closer to her face. He then leaned over and whispered against her ear. "Invite me in and I promise you won't be thinking at all."

And that was what she was afraid of.

She drew in a deep breath, thinking she would be

able to handle him. She opened the door and stepped back, hoping at that moment that she could.

What the hell am I doing here? Derringer wondered as he brushed by her. He had caught a whiff of her scent the moment she had opened the door, and as always it was playing hard on his senses.

He turned when he heard her close the door behind him and his gaze studied her. For some reason he didn't have the strength or inclination to tear his eyes away from her. What was wrong with him? When had he ever let a woman affect him this way? She was standing there leaning back against the door in her bare feet and a pair of leggings and a T-shirt. Her hair was back in that signature ponytail. She looked comfortable. She looked sexy. Damn, she looked good enough to eat.

He cleared his throat. "What are your plans for tonight?"

She shrugged. "I didn't have any. I was just going to watch a movie on Lifetime."

He was familiar with that channel, the one that was supposed to be for women that showed romance movies 24/7. His sisters used to be glued to their television sets, and in Bailey's case, sometimes to his.

"How would you like to go roller skating?"

The glow from a table lamp captured the expression of surprise on her face. "You want us to go out again?"

He noted that there was a degree of shock in her voice. There was a note of wariness as well.

"Yes, I know I should have called first, and I am sorry about that. And just to set the record straight, when I left home I didn't have a date. I didn't have any plans for tonight. I got in my car and I ended up here. What I said earlier was true. I needed to see you."

Serious doubt was etched in her features. "Why, Derringer? Why did you need to see me?"

It should be so easy to use this moment and come clean and say because I know who you are. I know you are the woman to whom I made love in what should have been a weak and crazy moment, but it ended up being the one time I slept with a woman that I remember the most. That no matter what I do or where I go, your scent is right there with me. You are responsible for the lust that rages through my body every time I think of you, whenever I see you. Even now there is a throbbing in my groin that you're causing and I want more than anything to make love to you again.

"Derringer?"

He realized at that moment that he hadn't answered her. Instead, he had been standing there and staring at her like a lust-crazed maniac. He slowly crossed the floor, pinning her in when he braced his hands on both sides of her head, and leaned in close to her mouth.

"I really don't know why I needed to see you tonight," he whispered huskily against her lips. "I can't explain it. I just needed to see you, be with you and spend time with you. I enjoyed Saturday night and—"

"Could have fooled me."

He noticed her voice had barely been audible, but he'd heard that, and he'd heard the hurt in her tone. He hadn't called her. He should have. He had wanted to. But he had fought the temptation. If only she knew to what degree he had fought it. A part of him knew being here with her now wasn't good; especially when he was thinking of all the things he wanted to do to her right now—against the door, on the floor, on her bed, the table, the sofa, every damn place in her house. But even more important was that he knew more about the situation than she did. He had yet to tell her that he knew about her visit to his home that night.

He had spent the last few days going over the video time and time again. It was evident from viewing the footage and seeing how she had merely stuck her head in the door that initially she'd had no intention of staying. Then she had glanced back at the box and decided to put it inside. She must have heard him fall once she was inside, because this week he remembered that part—missing the bed when he'd gotten up to use the bathroom and falling flat on his behind when he was returning to bed. He remembered someone, his Puddin' Tame, helping him back into bed, and the only thing he remembered after that was making love to a woman.

And the woman he had made love to had been her.

Things were still kind of fuzzy, but he remembered that much now. "I apologize for not calling you this week. I should have," he murmured.

She shook her head. "You didn't have to. I'm the one who should be apologizing. I should not have given you the impression that you should have called, just now."

His heart beat hard in his chest. That statement alone showed how different she was from the other women he messed around with. And that difference, among other things, he was convinced, was what had him here with her now.

"I don't want any apologies from you," he said,

leaning in closer, drawing one of her earlobes between his lips. "This is what I want." He then brushed his tongue across her lips and when she gave a sharp intake of breath, he did it again. And again.

"Why, Derringer...why me?" she whispered moments before she began trembling against the door.

"Why not you?" he breathed huskily against her lips before bending close to taste them again. Her flavor as well as her scent was getting to him on a level that made him want to push forward instead of drawing back.

Then deciding they had done enough talking for now, he sidled up closer to her and pressed his mouth to hers.

By rights she should send him away, Lucia's mind screamed over and over again. But it was hard to listen to what her mind was saying when Derringer was causing so much havoc with her body. This was the kind of kiss that could knock the sense out of a woman. It was long, deep and downright greedy. He was eating at her mouth as if it were his last meal, and there was no doubt in her mind this kiss was definitely X-rated.

And if that wasn't bad enough, his erection was pressing into her right at the juncture of her thighs, cradled against her womanly mound as if it had specifically sought out that part of her. And then there were the nipples of her breasts that were piercing his chest through the material of her T-shirt. She couldn't help but remember how it felt when they had been flesh to flesh, skin to skin. If he was seducing her then he was certainly going at it the right way.

He suddenly pulled back. Puzzled as to why, she

nervously chewed on her bottom lip—a lip he'd just released from devouring—and stared up at him. He was staring back. "I think we need to take time and think through a few things," he said huskily.

She arched a bemused brow. He evidently was speaking for himself. As far as she was concerned there was nothing to think through. She knew what she wanted and had a feeling that he did, too. So what was the problem? She knew the score. Nothing was forever with Derringer Westmoreland and she was okay with that. Although she was hopelessly in love with the man, she knew her limitations. She had accepted them long ago. She had made more strides within the last twelve days than she'd expected in her entire lifetime. They had made love, for heaven's sake, and he had kissed her senseless a week ago tomorrow.

But still…she was no longer a teenager with fantasies of him marrying her and living happily ever after with each other. She totally understood that was not the way the ball would bounce. She was not entering into anything with him blindly; she had both eyes wide open. Bottom line was that she didn't have to safeguard her heart. Although she wished otherwise, the man had her heart, lock, stock and barrel, and it was too late to do anything about it but gladly take whatever she could and live the rest of her life on memories.

"I think I need to give you time to get dressed so we can get to the skating rink."

She couldn't help but smile softly. "Do you really want to do that?"

He shook his head. "No, but if you knew what I really want to do you would probably kick me out."

"Try me."

He threw his head back and laughed. "No, I think I'll pass. I'll wait out here until you change clothes."

She moved around him to head down the hall and stopped right before crossing the threshold into her room. "You know it would probably be more fun if we stayed here, don't you?"

He smiled then said in a firm voice, "Go get dressed, Lucia."

Laughing, she entered the bedroom and closed the door behind her. While removing her clothes, Lucia made a decision about something.

For the first time ever she intended to try her luck at seducing a man.

Seven

Derringer glanced over at Lucia, who was across the room standing in line to check out their roller skates. He had two words to describe the jeans she was wearing—snug and tight. And then the first two words that would describe her overall appearance tonight were hot and sexy.

Deciding he needed to stop staring at her every chance he got, he glanced around. He had expected the place to be crowded since it was a Friday night, but why were there more kids than adults? Granted, it had been years since he'd gone skating, but still, he would think it was past these kids' bedtime.

He laughed recalling how some smart-mouthed preteen had come up to him a few minutes ago and said he hoped he and Lucia were fast enough on the skates to keep up and not get in anyone's way. Hell, he and Lucia weren't *that* old.

"What's so funny?"

He glanced down to see Lucia had returned with their skates. He then told her about the smart-mouthed kid and she smiled. "Doesn't this city still have a curfew?" he asked her.

She shook her head. "Not anymore."

He lifted a brow. "When did they do away with it?" He figured she would know because her dad had been a member of Denver's city council for years.

She smiled sweetly up at him. "They did away with it when Bane turned eighteen."

He stared at her for a second, saw she was serious and threw his head back and laughed so hard they couldn't help but get attention. "You're making a scene, Derringer Westmoreland," she whispered.

He shook his head and pulled her closer to him. "Is there anywhere Bane didn't leave his mark?"

"According to my father, the answer to that question is a resounding no. Now, come on, *old man,* or that kid will return and ask us to step aside."

He took her teasing of his age in stride, but still he reached out and grabbed her around the waist. "I'll show you who's old and who's not," he said, and then he took off, pulling her with him.

It was past three in the morning when Derringer returned Lucia home, and he smiled as he escorted her inside her home. It had taken a while, but he'd eventually shown that smart-mouthed kid why he once had earned the reputation of being hell on wheels with roller skates. And then when the kid had found out he was a Westmoreland—a cousin to the infamous Bane Westmoreland—he had to all but sign autographs.

"Can you believe those kids actually think Bane is some kind of hero?" he said, dropping onto Lucia's love seat.

She chuckled as she sat down on the sofa across from him. "Yes, I can believe that. Bane was bold enough to do some of the horrific things they would probably love to try but know that they can't get away with doing. Tell me, who in their right mind would take off in the sheriff's car while he's giving someone a ticket other than Bane? He became something of a legend if you were to read some of the stuff the girls wrote all over the walls in the bathroom at the local high school. He and the twins."

He glanced over at her. "How do you know about those walls? That was after your time."

She smiled as she settled back against the cushions, wrapping her arms across the back. "I have a young cousin who used to have a crush on Aidan and he's all she used to talk about then, in addition to all the trouble Aidan, Adrian and Bane would get into."

Derringer shook his head and chuckled, remembering those times. "And let's not forget Bailey—she was just as bad. At one time we considered sending all four of them to military school, but that would be like giving up on our own, and we knew we couldn't do that."

A serious expression touched his features before he said, "I don't tell Ramsey and Dillon enough how much I appreciate them keeping our family together. Losing my parents and my aunt and uncle at the same time was hard on everyone, but they helped us get through it." Derringer inwardly struggled with what he'd just told her, realizing he had never shared those emotions and feelings with anyone, certainly not any of his women.

"I'm sure they know you appreciate what they did, Derringer. The proof is in the successful, law-abiding men and women you all became. That's a testimony in itself. The Westmorelands are getting something now the townspeople figured they wouldn't ever get after your parents and aunt and uncle passed away."

He lifted a brow. "And what's that?"

"Respect." A smile touched her lips when she added, "And admiration. I wish you would have noticed the look on that kid's face tonight when he realized you were a Westmoreland."

Derringer snorted. "Yes, but he was admiring me for all the wrong reasons."

"It doesn't matter."

He knew deep down that Lucia was right—it didn't matter, because in the end what Dillon and Ramsey had done was indeed a success story in his book. He stretched his legs out in front of him thinking how throughout the evening he had enjoyed the time he was spending with Lucia. It had been the first time he'd spent with a woman when he'd had honest-to-goodness fun. She had been herself and hadn't gone out of her way to impress him and draw all the attention on her.

Even on the drive to and from the skating arena he had enjoyed their conversation, and although it was hard to believe, they had a lot in common and shared the same interests. They both enjoyed watching Westerns, they enjoyed a good comedy every once in a while and were huge fans of the Wayans brothers, Bill Cosby and

Sandra Bullock. She also rode horses and enjoyed going hunting.

But more than anything, he had enjoyed being with her, sharing her space and breathing the same air that she did. And he smiled, thinking she wasn't too bad on roller skates either. He had enjoyed going around the rink with her, often hearing her throaty laugh, looking over at her and seeing the huge smile on her face; and he especially liked wrapping his arms around her waist when they skated together.

"I had a wonderful time tonight, Derringer. I really enjoyed myself."

He glanced over at her. At some point, she had removed her boots and shifted position on the sofa to tuck her jeans-clad legs beneath her. But still, it didn't take much to remember how her long, curvy legs looked in a pair of shorts, a skirt or a dress. But most of all, he could recall those same legs wrapped around his waist while they had made love. The more time he spent with her, the more things were coming back to him that he had forgotten about their night together.

"I enjoyed myself as well," he responded.

"You were pretty good on those skates."

"You weren't so bad yourself." He wondered why he was sitting here making small talk with her when what he really wanted to do was to cross the room and join her on that sofa. His attention was trained directly on her and he could tell by the way she was moving her fingers on her knee he was making her nervous.

"Lucia, does my being here bother you?"

"What makes you think that?"

"Because you're over there and I'm here," he didn't

hesitate to say. He watched as she nervously licked her bottom lip, and immediately the lower part of his body—directly behind his zipper—responded in a hard-up way.

"There's nothing keeping you over there, Derringer," she said softly.

He couldn't help but smile at her deduction. She was right. There was nothing keeping him on this love seat when more than anything he wanted to be on that sofa with her. Knowing what he should do was stand up, thank her again for a good time and head toward the door and leave, never to return again, he remained seated for a minute. But he knew, just as much as he knew that tomorrow would bring another day, he wasn't going to do that.

And he also knew that she didn't know, she didn't have a clue just what she did to him, what being here with her was doing to him. He figured his intense attraction to her had everything to do with the night they had made love. But that wouldn't make sense since he'd made love to a number of women before and none had left the kind of lasting impression that she had. So why had the time with her been different, and why was he so quick to accept that it was?

The answer nearly made him tremble inside. It made his chest clench and made blood rush through his veins. She was deeply embedded in his system and he knew only one way to get her out of there. When they'd made love before, he hadn't been completely coherent and maybe that was the problem. Now he needed to make love to her in his right mind, if for no other reason than to purge her from his thoughts, mind and body. Then he could get on with his life and she could get on with hers. But before it was all over, he intended to let her know he was well aware that she had been his visitor that night.

Deciding he was doing too much thinking and not delivering enough action, he eased off the love seat.

Nowhere to run and nowhere to hide.

Deep down, Lucia knew she didn't want to do either as she watched Derringer slowly move toward her. Why was she getting all tense and nervous? Hadn't she made up her mind to seduce him tonight? But it seemed as if he had beat her to the punch and he was about to take things into his own hands. Literally.

His visit had been a surprise. She hadn't expected him tonight. He was the most unlikely person to show up at her place tonight or any other time. Not only had he shown up, but he'd taken her out again. Skating. It was their second date and he claimed the reason he was here was because he had needed to see her.

She knew needing to see her had only been a line and men like Derringer were good at saying such things. They said whatever they thought a woman wanted to hear. But that hadn't stopped her from allowing herself to be taken in, relish the moments spent with him and be greedy enough to want more. She would take whatever part of Derringer she could get. Tomorrow she would wake up and hate herself for being such a weakling where he was concerned, but she would also wake wearing the blush of a satisfied woman all over her face.

There was no doubt in her mind that he intended

to make love to her. He'd done it before, and from the dark, intense look in his eyes, he planned to do so again. And tonight he wouldn't get any resistance, because she loved him just that much and was secretly grateful for this time with him.

He slid down beside her on the sofa. "There is just something tantalizingly sweet about your scent, Lucia."

Another line, she was sure of it. "Is there?"

"Yes. It makes my body burn for you," he said, wrapping his arms around her shoulders.

She drew in a deep breath, thinking she would love to believe what he was saying, but knew better. However, tonight it was all about make-believe. Besides, it was hard not to melt under the intense look he was giving her and the way his arm felt around her shoulders. And he was sitting so close, every time he spoke his warm breath blew across her lips.

He then pulled back slightly and gazed at her thoughtfully. "You don't believe a word I've said, do you?"

She began nibbling on her bottom lip. She could easily lie and assure him that she did, but deep down she knew she didn't believe him. She tilted her chin upward. "Does it matter whether or not I believe you, Derringer?"

He continued to stare at her for a moment with an unreadable expression on his face, and for a split second she thought he was going to say something but he didn't. Instead, he reached out and cupped her chin with his fingertips before slowly lowering his mouth to hers.

Sensations ripped through her the moment their lips

touched. She closed her eyes when his tongue eased into her mouth and he began kissing her with a hunger that had her groaning deep in her throat.

Her heart thundered when he captured her tongue with his and began doing all kinds of erotic things to it, sucking on it as if there was a time limit to get his fill, mating their tongues as if all they had was the here and now. This was the kind of kissing that made a woman forget that she was supposed to be a lady.

She wanted this. She wanted every mind-blowing moment because she knew there *was* a time limit on this fantasy. Everyone around town knew of Derringer's reputation for getting tired of his women quickly. There was only a chosen one or two who were determined to hang in for the long haul no matter what—by their choice and not his. She refused to be one of those women. She would take this and be satisfied.

When he broke off the kiss to shift their positions to press her back against the sofa cushions, she moved willingly with him. She gazed up at him when his body eased on top of hers. She could feel his hard erection between her thighs.

He lowered his head and began nibbling around her throat, taking the tip of his tongue and licking around her chin. "Too many clothes." She heard him utter the word moments before he leaned up and, without warning, pulled the sweater over her head. He tossed it to the floor. He then proceeded to tug her jeans down her legs.

He looked down at her and smiled at her matching red lace bra and panties. She wondered what was going through his mind and why he was so captivated by her lingerie. He then glanced back up at her. "I like a woman who wears lace," he whispered huskily before leaning down and taking her mouth once more.

His lips seemed incredibly hot and he had no problem sliding his tongue where he pleased while kissing her with slow, deep strokes. And when she felt his fingers move toward her breasts, ease under her bra to stroke a nipple, she nearly shot off the sofa when sensations speared through her.

"Derringer…" she whispered in a strained voice.

This was getting to be too much and she began quivering almost uncontrollably, knowing what she'd heard for years was true. Derringer Westmoreland was almost too much for any woman to handle.

She was wrong. It did matter to him that she believed what he said.

That thought raged through Derringer's mind as he continued to kiss her with a hunger he could not understand. What was there about her that made him want to taste her all over, make her groan mercilessly and torture her over and over again before exploding inside her? The mere thought of doing the latter made his groin throb.

He pulled back slightly, wanting her to watch exactly what he was doing. What he was about to do. When he released the front fastener of her bra, his breath quickened when her breasts came tumbling out. They were full, firm and ripe and the nipples were dark and tightened even more into hard nubs before his eyes. And when he swooped his mouth down and captured a peak between his lips, she moaned and closed her eyes.

"Keep them open, Lucia. Watch me. I want you to see what I'm doing to you."

He saw her heavy-lidded eyes watch as he tugged a nipple into his mouth and begin sucking on it, and the more he heard her moan the more pressure he exerted with his mouth.

But that wasn't enough. Her scent was getting to him and he needed to touch her, to taste her, to bury himself in a feminine fragrance that was exclusively hers. He left one breast and went to another as he lowered a hand underneath the waistband of her lace bikini panties. And when his fingers ran over the wetness of her feminine folds, she writhed against his hand and let out a deep moan and whispered his name.

He lifted his head to stare down at eyes that were dazed with passion. "Yes, baby? You want something?"

Instead of answering, she began trembling as his fingers slipped inside her and he began stroking her while watching the display of emotions and expressions appear on her face. The breathless wonder drenched with pleasure that he saw in her gaze, in response to his touch, was a sight to behold and the sweetest thing he'd ever seen.

Lust thundered through him with the force of a hurricane and he knew he had to make love to her in the most primitive way. Leaning back, he eased to his feet and continued to hold her gaze while he tugged off his boots, pulled off his socks and unzipped his jeans. He took the time to remove a condom from the back pocket and held it between his teeth while he yanked down his jeans, careful of his engorged erection.

"Derringer…"

If she said his name like that, with that barely-there voice, one more time, he would lose it. The sound was sending splendorous shivers up his spine and there was a chance he would come the minute he got inside her, without making a single thrust. And he didn't want that. He wanted to savor the moment, make it last for as long as he could.

When he was totally naked, he stood before her and watched her gaze roam over him, seeing some parts of him that she probably hadn't seen their other night together. There was no shame in his game, but he knew deep down this wasn't a game with him. He was serious about what was taking place between them.

Thinking he had wasted more than enough time, he bent over her to remove the last item of clothing covering her body. Her panties. He touched the center of her and she sucked in a deep breath. He tossed aside the condom packet he'd been holding between his teeth. "You're drenched, baby," he said in a low, rough voice. "I know you don't believe me, but there is something about you that drives me crazy."

When he began tugging her panties down her legs, he whispered throatily, "Lift your hips and bend your legs for me."

She did, and when he removed her panties, instead of tossing them aside, he rubbed the lacy material over his face before he bent to the floor and tucked them into the back pocket of his jeans. He knew she was watching his every move and was probably wondering what on earth possessed him to do such a thing.

Instead of mounting her now, as he wanted to do,

there was something he wanted to do even more. Taste her. He wanted to taste all that sweetness that triggered the feminine aroma he enjoyed inhaling. It was a scent he was convinced he had become addicted to.

He lowered his body to his knees and before she could pull in her next breath, he pressed an open mouth to the wet, hot feminine lips of her sex. She groaned so deep in her throat that her body began trembling. But he kept focused on the pleasure awaiting him as he leisurely stroked her with his tongue, feasting on her with a hunger he knew she could not understand, but that he intended her to enjoy.

Because he was definitely enjoying it.

He'd been of the mind that no other woman had her scent. Now he was just as convinced that no other woman had her taste as well. It was unique. It was hers. And at the moment, as crazy as it sounded, he was also of the mind that it was also *his,* in a possessive way he'd never encountered before with any woman. The mere thought should have scared the hell out of him, but he was too far gone to give a damn.

When heat and lust combined and resonated off his mind he knew he had to be inside her or risk exploding then and there. He tore his mouth from her and threw his head back and released a deep savage groan. He then stared down at her while licking her juices from his lips. He felt as if he was taking part in a scorching-hot, exciting and erotic dream, and it was a dream he was dying to turn into a reality. And there was only one way he knew to do that.

He would take her and now.

Without saying a word, he leaned over and spread

her thighs and placed a kiss on each before moving off his knees to shift his body over hers. Instinctively she arched her back and wrapped her arms around his neck. Their gazes held as he eased his body down, the thick head of his shaft finding what it wanted and working its way inside her wet tightness. He paused when he'd made it halfway, glorying in the feel of her muscles clamping down on him, convulsing around him.

He wanted to take things slow, but the feel of her gripping him had him groaning deep in his throat, and when in a naughty, unexpected move she licked out her tongue and flicked his budded nipple before easing it into her mouth with a hungry suck, he took in a sharp breath at the same time he thrust hard into her.

When he heard her cry out, he apologized in a soothing whispered voice. "I'm sorry. I didn't mean to hurt you. Just lie still for a moment."

He used that time to lick around her mouth, nibble at the corners, and when she parted her mouth on a sweet sigh, he eased his tongue inside and sank right into a hungry kiss filled with more urgency and desire than he'd ever known or had ever cared knowing. Until now.

And then he felt the lower part of her body shift beneath the weight of his. He pulled back from the kiss. "That's it, baby," he crooned close to her ear. "Take it. All that you want."

His body remained still as she moved her body, grinding against him, dipping her hips into the sofa cushions before lifting them up again, arching her back in the process. Then she began rotating her hips, pushing up and lowering back down.

Derringer's body froze when he remembered the condom he'd tossed aside and he knew he needed to pull out now. But heaven help him, he couldn't do so. Being inside of her like this felt so darn right. He kept his body immobile until he couldn't stay still any longer and then he joined her, driving his erection deeper into her. He thrust in and out with precise and concentrated strokes that he felt all the way to the soles of his feet.

He had thought their first time together had been off the charts, but nothing, he decided, could compare to this. Nothing could compete with the incredible feeling of being inside her this way. Nothing. Desperate to reach the highest peak with her, he took total possession of her, kissing her with urgency while their bodies mated in the most primitive pleasure known to humankind.

He whispered erotic things in her ear before reaching down and cupping her face in his hands to stare down at her while his body continued to drive heatedly into hers. Their gazes locked and something happened between them at that moment that nearly threw him off balance. Somewhere in the back of his mind a voice was taunting that this had nothing to do with possessing but everything to do with claiming.

Denial froze hard in his throat and he wanted to scream that it wasn't possible. He claimed no woman. Instead, he grunted savagely as his body exploded, and then he heard her scream as she cried out in ecstasy. He kept thrusting into her, pushing them further and further into sweet oblivion and surging them beyond the stars.

Eight

Lucia moved her head slowly, opened her eyes and then came fully awake when a flash of sunlight through her bedroom window hit her right in the face. It was then that she felt the male body pressed tightly against her back and the heated feel of Derringer's breathing on her neck.

She then remembered.

They had made love on the sofa before moving into her bedroom where they had made love again before drifting off to sleep. Sometime during the wee hours of early morning they had made love again. The entire thing seemed unreal, but Derringer's presence in her bed assured her that it had been real.

Her body felt sore, tender in a number of places, but mostly between her legs, and she wouldn't be surprised if her lips were swollen from all the kissing they had done. Her cheeks flooded with heat thinking about a number of other things they'd gotten into as well. She had proven to him in a very sexual way that she definitely knew how to ride a stallion. He had taunted her to prove it and she'd done so.

Her eyes fluttered closed as she thought how she would handle things from here on out. She knew last night meant more to her than it had to him, and she could handle that. But what she wouldn't be able to handle was letting things go beyond what they'd shared these past few hours. She loved him and for him to ever make love to her again would turn things sexual, into a casual relationship that would tarnish her memories rather than enhance them. She was smart enough to know when to let go and move on. Now was the time.

Tears flooded her eyes. Derringer would always have her heart, but the reality was that she would never have his. And being the type of person that she was, she could never allow herself to become just one in a long line of women vying for his attention. She preferred letting things go back to the way they were between them before they'd become intimate.

The way she saw things, if she never had him then there was no way she could lose him. She couldn't risk a broken heart because of Derringer and she knew her place in his life. She didn't have one. If she began thinking of developing something serious with him knowing the kind of man he was, she was setting herself up for pain from which she might never be able to heal.

She would continue to love him like this—secretly. She had gotten used to doing things that way and, no matter what, she couldn't let their sexual encounters—no matter how intense they'd been—fill her head and mind with false illusions.

She swallowed when she felt Derringer's penis swell against her backside and tried to convince herself it wouldn't be a good idea to make love to him one last time. But she knew the moment he pulled her closer to his hard, masculine body that she would. This would be saying goodbye to the intimacy between them. She knew it even if he didn't.

"You're awake?" He turned her in his arms to face him.

Desire rippled through her the moment she looked into his face. Propped with his head on her pillow, his eyes had the same desire-glazed look they'd had that first night they'd made love. It was a sexy, drowsy look, complete with a darkened shadow on his chin. No man had a right to look this good in the morning. He looked so untamed, wild and raw. His rumpled look was calling out to her, arousing her and making her want him all over again.

"Sort of," she said, yawning, and couldn't help the anticipation she heard in her voice. And when he gave her a dimpled cowboy smile, sensations shot through her entire body, but especially in the area between her thighs.

"Then let me wake you up the Derringer West-moreland way." He then captured her mouth at the same time he tossed his leg over hers, adjusting their positions to ease inside her body.

"Oh," she whispered, and when he locked his leg on her and began slowly moving in and out of her and capturing her lips with his, she figured there was nothing wrong with one for the road…even though she knew she would end up in heaven.

Derringer's smile faded as he buttoned up his shirt and stared at Lucia. "What do you mean we can't ever make love again?"

He saw the flash of regret that came into her eyes before she stopped brushing her teeth long enough to rinse out her mouth. "Just what I said, Derringer. Last night was special and I want to remember it that way."

He was confused. "And you don't think you can if we make love again?"

"No. I know about the women you usually sleep with and, personally, I don't want to be one of them."

He frowned, crossing his arms over his chest, not sure he liked what she'd said. "Then why did you sleep with me last night?"

"I had my reasons."

His frown deepened. He couldn't help but wonder if those reasons were the same ones he had initially suspected her of having. And it didn't help matters to know that every time he had made love to her they had been unprotected. The first time had been a slip-up, and then after that, he'd deliberately chosen not to think about it. Why he'd done such a thing, he didn't know. He usually made it a point to always use protection. Even now, Lucia might be pregnant with his child.

"And just what are those reasons, Lucia?"

"I'd rather not say."

Anger ignited inside him. That response wasn't good enough.

"Oh!" she cried out in surprise when he reached

out, snatched her off her feet and tossed her over his shoulders like a sack of potatoes and strode out of the bathroom.

"Derringer! What in the world is wrong with you? Put me down."

He did. Tossing her on the bed and glaring down at her. "I want to hear these reasons."

She glared back. "You don't need to know them. All you need to know is that I won't be sharing a bed with you again."

"Why? Because you think you're pregnant now and that's what this is about?"

Shock leaped into her face. "Pregnant? What are you talking about?"

"Are you on the pill or something?"

He could tell his question had surprised her. "No."

His frown deepened. "There's only one reason I can think of for a woman to let a man come inside her. Are you going to deny that sleeping with me this time around…as well as the last time…has nothing to do with you wanting a Westmoreland baby?"

He saw her throat tighten. "The last?"

"Yes," he said between clenched teeth. "I know all about your little visit that night when I was drugged up on pain medication."

She blinked. "You know?"

"Yes, and I couldn't figure out why you, a virgin, would get into my bed and take advantage of me. And, yes, I do remember you were a virgin even if I couldn't recall your identity."

She angrily reared up on her haunches. "I did not take advantage of you! I was helping you back into bed after you fell. If anything, you're the one who took advantage of me."

"So you say." He could see fury consume her body. and smoke was all but coming out her ears, but he didn't care.

She rolled off the bed and stood in front of him, almost nose to nose. "Are you insinuating I slept with you that night to deliberately get pregnant? And that I only slept with you last night and this morning for the same reason?"

"What am I supposed to think?"

She threw her hair over her shoulders. "That maybe I am different from all those other women you spend your time with, and that I would not have an ulterior motive like that," she all but screamed at him.

"You said you had your reasons."

"Yes, I have my reasons and they have nothing to do with getting pregnant by you, but everything to do with being in love with you. Do you have any idea how it is to fall in love with a man knowing full damn well he won't ever love you back?"

"In love with me," he said in a shocked stupor. "Since when?"

"Since I was sixteen."

"Sixteen!" He shook his head. "Hell, I didn't know."

She placed her hands on her hips and her eyes sparked with fire. "And you weren't *supposed* to know. It was a secret I had planned to take to my grave. Then like a fool I rushed over to your place when I heard you'd gotten hurt. And when you fell, I rushed up the stairs to help you back into bed and you wouldn't get off me."

He lifted a brow. His head was still reeling from her admission of love. "Are you saying I forced myself on you?"

"No, but I would not have gotten into bed with you if you hadn't fallen on top of me. And then, when you began kissing me, I—"

"Didn't want me to stop," he finished for her. Her cheeks darkened and he knew he'd embarrassed her. "Look, Lucia, I—"

"No, *you* look, Derringer. You're right. The thought of pushing you off me only entered my mind for a quick second, but I didn't set out to get pregnant by you that night or any other night."

"But you let me make love to you without any protection." He remembered all too well that he hadn't used a condom this time either.

"Then I can accuse you of the same thing. Trying to *get* me pregnant," she all but snarled.

"And why would I do something like that?"

"I don't know, but if you're willing to think the worst of me, then I can certainly do the same thing with you. You had taken the condom out of your wallet last night, why didn't you put it on?"

Derringer tensed. To say he'd been too carried away with making love to her would be to admit a weakness for her that he didn't want to own up to. "I think this conversation has gotten out of hand."

"You're right. I want you to leave."

He arched his brow. "Leave?"

"Yes. And my front door is that way," she said as she pointed to the door.

He narrowed his eyes. "I know where your door is located and we haven't finished our conversation."

"There's nothing else left to say, Derringer. I've already told you more than I should have and I'm ashamed of doing it. Now that you know how I feel, I won't let you take advantage of those feelings. For me it's even more important to protect my heart more than ever. Nothing has changed from the way you've always looked at me. Most of the time you acted like I didn't exist."

"That's not true. I told you I was attracted to you a few years back."

"Yes, and I honestly thought it meant something and that you were seeking me out after all that time. Now I know you only did so because you knew I was the one who slept with you that night."

She didn't say anything for a moment and then asked, "How did you know? I figured you wouldn't remember anything."

He jammed his hands into his jeans. "Oh, I remembered just fine, and you left a little something behind that definitely jogged my memory. Something pink and lacy. I just couldn't remember who they belonged to. My security system gave me the answers I needed. I had video cameras installed outside my place last month. You were the woman I saw entering my house that evening and the same one I saw sneaking out the next morning with a made-love-all-night-long look all over you."

Lucia tightened her bathrobe around her. "Like I said, that wasn't the purpose of my visit. I just wanted to make sure you were okay."

"It had been storming that night. You hate storms. Yet you came to check on me," he said.

That realization touched something within him. The reason he knew about her aversion to storms was because of something Chloe had once teased her about from their college days in Florida that involved a torrential thunderstorm and her reaction to it.

"Doesn't matter now."

"And what if I say it matters to me?" he all but snarled.

"Then I would suggest you get over it," she snapped back.

"I can't. I want to be with you again."

She narrowed her gaze. "And I told you that we won't be together that way ever again. So get it through that thick head of yours that I won't become just another woman you sleep with. You have enough of those."

Emotions he had never felt before stirred in Derringer's stomach. He should leave and not come back and not care if he ever saw her again, but for some reason she had gotten in his blood and making love to her again hadn't gotten her out. Instead the complete opposite had happened; she was more in his blood than ever before.

"I'll give you time to think about what I said, Lucia." He turned to leave the room knowing she was right on his heels as he moved toward the living room.

"There's nothing to think about," she snapped behind him.

He turned back around after snagging his Stetson off the rack. "Sure there is. We will be making love again."

"No, we won't!"

"Yes, we will," he said, moving toward the door. "You're in my blood now."

"I'm sure so are a number of other women in this town."

There was no point in saying that although he'd had a lot of women in the past, none had managed to get into his blood before. When he got to the door, he put on his hat before turning back to her. "Get some rest. You're going to need it when we make love again."

"I told you that we—"

He leaned forward and swiped whatever words she was about to say from her lips with a kiss, effectively silencing her. He then straightened and smiled at the infuriated face staring back at him and tipped the brim of his hat. "We'll talk later, sweetheart."

He opened the door and stepped outside and it didn't bother him one bit when she slammed the door behind him with enough force to wake up the whole neighborhood.

Chloe leaned forward and kissed Lucia on the cheek. "Hey, cheer up. It might not be so bad."

Lucia covered her face with both hands. "How can you say that, Clo? Now that Derringer knows how I feel, he's going to do everything in his power to find a weakness to get me back in his bed. I should never have told him."

"But you did tell him, so what's next?"

She lowered her hands and narrowed her eyes. "Nothing is next. I know what he's after and it's not happening. And just to think he knew I was the one who slept with him that night, when silly me thought he didn't have a clue. And now he wants to add me to his list."

Chloe raised a brow. "Did he actually say that?"

"He didn't have to. His arrogance was showing and that was enough." She doubted she could forget his exit and his statement about their talking later. She was so angry with him. The only good part about his leaving was the mesmerizing view of his backside before she slammed the door shut on him.

"I've known Derringer a lot longer than you, Chloe, and he doesn't know the meaning of committing to one woman," she decided to add.

Chloe shrugged. "Maybe he's ready to change his ways."

Lucia rolled her eyes. "Fat chance."

"I don't know," Chloe said, tapping her finger against her chin. "Of the three die-hard-bachelor Westmoreland men who hang tight most of the time—Jason, Zane and Derringer—I think Jason will get married first…then Derringer…and last, Zane." She chuckled. "I can see Zane kicking, screaming and throwing out accusations all the way to the altar."

Lucia couldn't help but smile because she could envision that as well. Zane was more of a womanizer than Derringer. Jason didn't have the reputation the other two had, but he was still considered a ladies' man around town because he didn't tie himself down to any one woman.

"Derringer is so confident he's getting me back into his bed again, but I'm going to show him just how wrong he is."

Chloe took a long sip of her iced tea. She had been out shopping and had decided to drop by Lucia's. Unfortunately, she had found her best friend in a bad mood and it didn't take long for her to get Lucia to spill her guts about everything.

"Now, tell me once more your reason for not wanting to sleep with Derringer again."

Lucia rolled her eyes as she sat back on the sofa. "I know how those Westmoreland brothers and cousins operate with women. I don't want to become one of those females, pining away and sitting by the phone hoping I'm next on the list to call."

"But you've been pining away for Derringer for years anyway."

"I haven't been pining. Yes, I've loved him, but I knew he didn't love me back and I accepted that. I was fine with it. I had a life. I didn't expect him to phone or show up on my doorstep making booty calls."

Chloe laughed. "He didn't make a booty call exactly. He did take you out on a date."

"But that's beside the point."

Chloe leaned forward, grinning. "And what is your point exactly? I warned you that once you had a piece of a Westmoreland you'd become addicted. Now you've had Derringer more than once, so watch out. Staying away from him is going to be easier said than done, Lucia."

Lucia shook her head. "You just don't understand, Chloe."

Chloe smiled sadly. "You're right, I don't. I don't understand how a woman who loves a man won't go after him using whatever means it takes to get him. What are you afraid of?"

Lucia glanced over at Chloe. "Failing. Which will lead to heartbreak." She drew in a deep breath. "I had a cousin who had a nervous breakdown over a man. She was twenty and her parents sent her all the way from Nashville to live with us for a while. She was simply pathetic. She would go to bed crying and wake up doing the same thing. It was so depressing. I hate to say this, but I couldn't wait until she pulled herself together enough to leave."

"How sad for her."

"No, that's the reality of things when you're dealing with a man like Derringer."

Chloe quirked a brow. "I still think you might be wrong about him."

Lucia figured she couldn't change the way her best friend thought; however, she intended to take all the precautions where Derringer was concerned. Now he saw her as a challenge because she was the woman not willing to give him the time of day anymore.

Some men didn't take rejection well and she had a feeling that Derringer Westmoreland was one of them.

Nine

Jason snapped his fingers in front of Derringer's face. "Hey, man, have you been listening to anything I've said?"

Derringer blinked, too ashamed to admit that he really hadn't. The last thing he recalled hearing was something about old man Bostwick's will being read that day. "Sort of," he said, frowning. "You were talking about old man Bostwick's will."

Herman Bostwick owned the land that was adjacent to Jason's. For years, Bostwick had promised Jason if he ever got the mind to sell, he would let Jason make him the first offer. The man died in his sleep and had been laid to rest a couple of days ago. It didn't take much to detect from the look in Jason's eyes that he wanted the land and Hercules, Bostwick's prize stallion. A colt from Hercules would be a dream come true for any horse breeder.

"So who did he leave the land to?" Derringer asked. "I hope it didn't go to his brother. Kenneth Bostwick is one mean son of a gun and will take us to the cleaners if we have to buy the land and Hercules from him."

Jason shook his head and took a sip of his beer. "The old man left everything to his granddaughter. Got Kenneth kind of pissed off about it."

Derringer lifted a brow. "His granddaughter? I didn't know he had one."

"It seems not too many people did. I understand that he and his son had a falling-out years ago, and when he left for college the son never returned to these parts. He married and settled down in the South. He had one child, a girl."

Derringer nodded and took a sip of his own beer. "So this granddaughter got the land and Hercules?"

"Yes. The only good thing is that I heard she's a prissy miss from Savannah who probably won't be moving here permanently. More than likely she'll be open to selling everything, and I want to be ready to buy when she does."

Jason then slid down to sit on the steps across from him, and Derringer looked out across his land. It was late afternoon and he still couldn't get out of his mind what had happened earlier that day with Lucia. If she thought he was done with her then she should think again.

He glanced over at his cousin. "Have you ever met a woman that got in your blood, real good?"

Jason just stared at him for a long moment. It didn't take much to see that Derringer's question had caught his cousin off guard. But he knew Jason; he liked mulling things over—sometimes too damn long.

"No. I'm not sure that can happen. At least not with me. Any woman who gets in my blood will end up being the one I marry. I don't have a problem with settling down and getting married one day, mind you. One day, when I'm ready, I want to start a family. I want to will everything I've built up to my wife and kids. You know what they say, 'You can't take it with you.'"

Jason then studied Derringer. "Why do you ask? Have you met a woman that's gotten deep in your blood?"

Derringer glanced away for a moment and then returned his gaze to Jason. "Yes...Lucia."

"Lucia Conyers?"

"Yeah."

Jason stood, almost knocking over his beer bottle. "Damn, man, how do you figure that? You only had one date with her."

Derringer smiled. "I've had two. We went skating last night." He didn't say anything and wanted to see what Jason had to say. Jason sat back down without opening his mouth.

"She's different," Derringer added after a moment.

Jason glanced over at him. "Of course she's different. You're not talking about one of your usual airheads or Derringer's Pleasers. We're discussing Lucia Conyers, for heaven's sake. She used to be one of the smartest girls at her school. Remember when Dillon and Ramsey paid her to tutor Bailey that time so she wouldn't be left back? Lucia was only seventeen then."

Derringer smiled. He had almost forgotten about that time. And if he wanted to believe what she'd told him earlier, she had been in love with him even then. "Yes, I remember."

"And remember the time Megan got her first A on a science project because she was smart enough to team up with Lucia?"

Derringer chuckled, recalling that time as well. "Yeah, I recall that time as well." At least he did now.

"And you actually think someone that smart is destined to be your soul mate?"

"Soul mate?"

"Yes, if a woman is in your blood that much then it means she's destined to be your soul mate. Someone you want to be with all the time. Think about it, Derringer. Like I said, Lucia is not some airhead, she's pretty smart."

He didn't say anything for a moment as he studied his boots, grinning, thinking Jason's question had to be a joke. Then he lifted his gaze to find a serious-looking Jason staring at him, still waiting for a response. So he gave him the only one he knew. "Yes, I'm not exactly a dumb ass, Jason, so what does her being so smart have to do with anything? And as far as being my soul mate if that means sharing a bed with her whenever I want, then I intend to do everything in my power to convince her that she is the one."

Jason rolled his eyes and then rubbed his chin thoughtfully as he stared at Derringer. "So are you saying you've fallen in love with Lucia?"

Derringer looked taken aback. "Fallen in love with her? Are you crazy? I wouldn't go *that* far."

Jason appeared confused. "You have no problem

wanting to claim her as your soul mate and sleep with her, but you aren't in love with her?"

"Yes. That's pretty much the shape and size of it."

Jason shook his head, grinning. "I hate to tell you this, but I'm not sure that's how it works."

Derringer finished off his beer and said, "Too bad. That's the way it's going to work for me."

On Monday morning, Lucia stood in the middle of her office refusing to let the huge arrangement of flowers get to her. They were simply gorgeous and she would be the first to admit Derringer had good taste. But she knew just what the flowers represented. He wanted her back in his bed and would try just about anything to get her there. She wished things could go back to how they used to be when he hadn't had a clue about her feelings. But it was too late for that.

Six hours later, Lucia glanced over at the flowers and smiled. They were just as beautiful as they had been when they'd been delivered that morning. She glanced at her watch. She would leave in a couple of hours to go straight to class. Mondays were always her busiest days with meetings and satellite conference calls with the other *Simply Irresistible* offices around the country during the day and class at night.

She kicked off her shoes, leaned back in her chair and closed her eyes. The office would be closing in less than twenty minutes and since she would be there long after that, she figured there was no reason she couldn't grab a quick nap.

With her eyes shut, it didn't surprise her when an image of Derringer came into view. Boy, he was gorgeous. And arrogant. She frowned, thinking he was as arrogant as he was gorgeous Still…

She wasn't sure how long she slept. But she remembered she was dreaming of Derringer, and wherever they were, she had whispered for him to kiss her and he had. She heard herself moan as the taste of him registered on her brain, and she couldn't help thinking how real her dream was. And was that really the feel of his fingertips on her chin as he devoured her mouth with plenty of tongue play. She could actually inhale his scent. Hot, robust and masculine.

They continued kissing in her dream and she simply melted while he leisurely explored the depths of her mouth. Nobody could kiss like him, she thought as he probed his tongue deeper. She had dreamed of him kissing her many times before, but for some reason this was different. This was like the real deal.

Her eyes flew open and she squealed when she realized it wasn't a dream! It was the real deal! She jerked forward and pushed him away from her. "Derringer! How dare you come into my office and take advantage of me."

He stood back, licked his lips and smiled. "The way I assume you took advantage of me that night? Just for the record, Lucia, you asked me to kiss you. When I entered your office, you were whispering my name. And I distinctively heard you ask me to kiss you."

"I was dreaming!"

He gave her an arrogant smirk. "Nice to know I'm in your dreams, sweetheart."

She eased out of her chair and crossed her arms over her chest. When she saw where his gaze went—directly to where her blouse dipped to reveal more cleavage than she wanted—she dropped her arms, scowling. "What are you doing here and who let you into my office?"

He jammed his hands into the pockets of his jeans. "I came to see you and I arrived when your administrative assistant was leaving. She remembered me from Chloe and Ramsey's wedding and let me in."

His smile widened. "She figured I was safe. I did knock on the door a few times before I entered, and would not have come in if I hadn't heard you call out my name."

Lucia swallowed. Had she really called out his name? She ignored that possibility. "Why are you here?"

"To make sure you liked your flowers."

She dragged her gaze from him to the huge floral arrangement she had been admiring all day. In fact, everyone in the office had admired it, and she knew they were wondering who'd sent the flowers. She glanced back at Derringer. Okay, maybe she should have called and thanked him; she hadn't wanted to give him any ideas, but it seemed he'd gotten plenty without her help.

"Yes, they're beautiful. Thank you. Now you can leave."

He shook his head. "I figured while I'm here I might as well drop you off at school. You do have class tonight, right?"

"Yes, but why would I want you to drop me off at school when I can drive myself? I do have a car."

"Yes, but I wouldn't want you to get a ticket. You told me all about your Monday-night professor and how he hates it when anyone is late. You also mentioned that tonight is your final. You're going to be late."

Lucia glanced down at her watch and went still. She wasn't aware she had slept that long. She needed to be in class in twenty minutes and it would take her longer than that to get through town. Professor Turner had already warned the class that he would close his door exactly at seven, and Derringer was right, tonight she was to take her final.

She slipped into her shoes and quickly moved around the desk to grab her purse out of the desk drawer. "And just how are you supposed to get me there any sooner than I can drive myself?" she asked, hurrying out the office door. He was right behind her.

"I have my ways." He then pulled his cell phone out of his back pocket. "Pete? This is Derringer. I need a favor."

She glanced over her shoulder as she was locking the door. He was calling Pete Higgins, one of the sheriff's deputies and also one of his good friends.

"I need escort service from *Simply Irresistible* to the U, and we need to be there in less than fifteen minutes." Derringer smiled. "Okay, we're on our way down."

He glanced over at her when he put his phone in his back pocket. "We'll leave your car here and come back for it after class."

She frowned over at him as they stepped into the elevator. "Why can't I drive my own car and your friend Pete can just give me escort service?"

He shook his head. "It doesn't work that way. He knows I'm trying to impress my girl."

"I am not your girl, Derringer."

"Sure you are. Why else would you moan my name in your sleep?"

Lucia turned her head away from him, deciding that question didn't need an answer. Besides, what response could she give him?

Once they reached the bottom floor, things moved quickly. He took her laptop bag off her shoulder and put it in the backseat of his truck. By the time he escorted her to the passenger side, Pete pulled up in the patrol car with his lights flashing and a huge grin on his face. He nodded at her before giving Derringer a thumbs-up.

Luckily, she got to school in one piece and was able to make it to class on time. An hour or so later, after she'd finished her exam and placed her pencil aside, instead of glancing back over her exam to make sure she didn't need to do any last-minute changes, her mind drifted to Derringer.

Lucia shook her head. What some men wouldn't do for a piece of tail, she thought. Regardless of what Chloe assumed, she knew that was probably all she was to him. Of course he was trying to impress her just to prove a point, and just the thought that he had caught her dreaming about him, and that in her sleep she had asked him to kiss her, was enough for her to wear a brown bag over her head for the rest of the year.

And what was even worse was that he would be picking her up when class was over. She had no choice if she wanted to get home without taking the bus. A part of her steamed at the thought of how things had worked out nicely for him in that regard. He would be driving her to get her car and nothing more. If he thought there would be more, he had another think coming.

The moment she stepped out of the Mass Communications Building, she glanced around. Derringer's truck was parked in a space in a lighted area and he was leaning against it as if he was expecting her, which was odd since he hadn't known when her class would let out. Had he been here the entire time?

She quickly crossed to where he stood. "How did you know I was about to walk out?"

He glanced over at her as he opened the truck door for her. "I didn't. I figured that you would catch a cab to get your car if I wasn't here, so I thought the best thing to do was to be here when you came out."

She frowned at him before stepping up into the truck. "You've been here the whole time?"

"Yep."

"Don't you have anything better to do?" she asked coolly.

"Nope." He then closed the door and moved around the front of the truck to get into the driver's side.

He closed the door, buckled his seat belt and turned the key in the ignition. "Don't you think you're getting carried away with all this, Derringer?"

He chuckled. "No."

She rolled her eyes. "Seriously. I couldn't have been that great in bed."

His mouth tilted in a slow, ultrasatisfied smile. "Trust me, Lucia. You were."

She crossed her arms over her chest as he pulled out of the parking lot. "So you admit this is only about sex."

"I didn't say that, so I won't be admitting anything. I told you what I wanted."

She glanced over at him. "To sleep with me again."

"Yes, but not just a couple more times. I'm talking about the rest of my life. You're my soul mate." Derringer smiled thinking that sounded pretty darn good and had to thank Jason for putting the idea into his head.

Her mouth dropped. "Soul mate?"

"Yes."

"That's insane," she threw out

"That's reality. Get used to it," he threw back.

She turned around in her seat as much as her seat belt would allow. "It's not reality and I won't get used to it, because it doesn't make sense. If this has anything to do with you thinking I got pregnant from our previous encounters you don't have that to worry about. My monthly visitor arrived this morning."

"That wasn't it, although that would have definitely been important to me if you had gotten pregnant. But like I told you before, you're in my blood now. You were a virgin and I'd never been with a virgin before."

"Whoop-de-do," she said sarcastically. "No big deal."

"For me it is."

She just stared at him, deciding not to argue with him anymore. Doing so would give her a friggin' headache. She shifted positions to sit straight in her seat and closed her eyes, but she wouldn't go to sleep for fear of waking up with her lips locked to his again.

Each time she felt herself being lulled to sleep by the smooth jazz sounds coming from the CD player, she would open her eyes to gaze out the window and study all the buildings they passed. She thought Denver was a beautiful city and there was no other place quite like it.

Due to the lack of traffic, they returned to her office building sooner than she had anticipated. And, she tried convincing herself, not as quickly as she would have liked. But she knew that was a lie. She liked the fact that she was the woman riding in the truck with him tonight. She had been the one he had waited for outside her classroom building. And she was the one for whom he had ordered a special escort service to get her to school on time. Then there were the flowers. A girl could really succumb to him if she wasn't careful.

"How do you think you did on your test tonight?"

His question surprised her and she glanced over at him when he parked his truck behind her car. She couldn't help but smile. "I think I aced it. I'm almost sure of it. There were a lot of multiple-choice questions, but there was one essay question to test our writing skills."

"I'm happy for you then."

"Thanks."

She watched as he opened his door and then walked around the back of the truck to open the door for her. Once he helped her out, they stood there facing each other. "I appreciate all you did tonight, Derringer. Because of you I got to school on time."

"No problem, baby."

The term of endearment sent sensations rippling through her. "Don't call me that, Derringer."

"What?"

"Baby."

He leaned against his truck. "Why?"

"Because I'm sure I'm not the only woman you've called that."

"No, you're not, but you're the only one I've called that when it meant something."

She shook her head as she walked slowly to her car with him strolling beside her. The April air was cold and everyone was talking about a snowstorm headed their way this weekend. "You just won't give up, will you?"

"No."

"I wish you would."

They came to a stop next to her car. The smile he gave her was slow and sexy. "And I wish you would let me make love to you again, Lucia."

She was certain that irritation showed on her face. "Yet you want me to believe it's not just about sex?"

She shook her head sadly, thinking he just didn't get it. She loved him and now that he knew how she felt, she refused to settle for anything less than being loved in return. She knew for him to fall in love with her was something that wouldn't happen—not in her wildest dreams—so all she wanted to do was get on with her life without him being a part of it. "Good night, Derringer."

He moved out of the way when she got into her car and quickly drove away.

Later that night, Derringer tossed and turned in his bed. Finally, he pulled himself up and reached out to turn on the light. Brightness flooded the room and he rubbed his hands down his face.

Tomorrow would be a busy day for Denver's branch

of D&M Horse-Breeding and Training Company. In fact, the rest of the week would be hectic. His cousin Cole would be delivering more than one hundred horses from Texas at the end of the week and they needed to make sure everything was ready. It didn't help matters that a snowstorm was expected this weekend. That made things even more complicated as well as challenging.

He reached behind him and lifted his pillow and smiled when his hand touched the lacy items. He had two pairs of Lucia panties. Added to the pink pair were the red ones he'd taken off her last weekend. He wondered if she'd missed them yet and figured she probably hadn't; otherwise, she would have mentioned it.

And she wasn't pregnant. He'd actually been disappointed when she'd made that announcement. He had gotten used to the idea that perhaps she could be pregnant with his child. He knew that kind of thinking didn't make much sense, but he had.

He settled back down in bed thinking she just wouldn't let up with this "only sex" thing. He had all but told her she was his soul mate so what else did she want?

He knew the answer without thinking much about it. She wanted him to love her, but that wouldn't and couldn't happen. What if she got real sick or something and he couldn't get her to the hospital in time? What if she was in a car accident and didn't survive? What if she got stampeded by a herd of horses? What if…he lost her like he had his parents? His aunt and uncle? They were here one day and had been gone the next. He rubbed his hand down his face, not liking how his thoughts were going. He was freaking out for no reason; especially when he didn't intend to get attached to her like that.

He liked things just the way they were and didn't intend for any woman, not even Lucia, to start messing with his mind…and definitely not with his heart. But he wanted her.

There had to be a middle ground for them, something they could both agree on. It would have to be something that would satisfy them both.

He would come up with a plan. Because, no matter what, he had no intention of giving up on her.

Ten

Lucia closed the lid to her washing machine and leaned back against it thinking that Derringer had not given her back the panties he'd taken off her the other night. The red pair. Now he had two. What was he doing with them? Collecting them as souvenirs?

She strolled to the window and glanced out. It looked totally yucky outside. The forecasters' predictions had been correct. She had awakened to see huge snowflakes falling outside. That's the only thing she missed about the time she lived in Florida. This was the middle of April, spring break in most states and it was hard to believe that in some other place the sun was shining brightly. A week spent on Daytona Beach sounded pretty darn good about now. At least the snow had waited for the weekend and most people didn't have a reason to venture outside.

Her parents had gotten smart and decided to fly to Tennessee for a few weeks to visit her mother's sister. Chloe had called this morning to chat and to tell her how she, Ramsey and the baby were snuggled inside in front of the roaring fireplace and planned to stay that way. Lucia sighed deeply, thinking this was the only time she regretted being an only child. Things could get lonely at times.

She moved away from the window to go into the kitchen to make herself a cup of hot chocolate and watch that movie she had planned to watch last week, and she remembered why she hadn't.

Derringer had dropped by.

She hadn't heard from him since the night he had taken her to school. Maybe he had finally admitted to himself that he only wanted one thing from her and had moved on to some other willing female. The thought of him making love to someone else had her hurting inside, but she could deal with it the way she'd always done. It wasn't the first time she'd known the man she loved was sleeping with others and it wouldn't be the last. But it hurt knowing someone else was the recipient of his smile, his look and his touch. More than anything, a part of her wished she hadn't experienced any of it for herself. But then a part of her was glad that she had and would not trade in a single moment.

Moments later, with a cup of hot chocolate in her hand, she moved toward the living room to watch her movie. She had a fire blazing in the fireplace and it added soothing warmth to the entire room. Why she wanted to watch a romantic movie when she lacked romance in her own life was beyond her. But then, women had their dreams and fantasies, didn't they?

Lucia had settled back against her sofa with a cup in one hand and a remote in the other when the doorbell rang. She frowned, wondering what on earth could get Mrs. Noel to come across the street in this weather, unless her heating unit was on the blink again. Standing, she placed the cup and the remote on the table and headed for the door. She looked out the peephole and caught her breath.

Derringer!

Denying the rush of heat she immediately felt between her thighs, seeing him standing there and looking sexier than any man had a right to look—this time of day and in this horrid weather—she drew in a deep breath and fought the anger escalating in her chest. She would not hear from him for a week or so and then he would show up at her place unannounced. It didn't matter that she had told him to leave her alone. That was beside the point. The only point she could concentrate on was that he evidently thought he could add her to his booty-call list. Well, she had news for him.

She snatched the door open and was about to ask what he was doing there, but wasn't given the chance to do so.

Derringer didn't give Lucia the chance to ask any questions, but leaned in and covered her mouth with his. He not only wanted to silence her, he also wanted the heat from his kiss to inflame her as they stood just inside with a frigid snowstorm raging outside. There was no doubt in his mind the kiss had enough spark, power and electricity to light the entire city of Denver. And he felt it all rush through his body.

She didn't resist him, and at the moment that was a good thing. He didn't need her resistance, what he needed was this—the taste of her all over his tongue.

He had tried not thinking about her all week. Hell, with the delivery of those horses he'd had enough to keep his mind and time occupied. But things hadn't happened quite that way. She'd still managed to creep into his thoughts most of the time, and he had awakened that morning with a need to see her so intense that he just couldn't understand it. And nothing, not elephant snowflakes nor below-zero-degree temperature would keep him from her. From this.

He finally pulled back from the kiss. Somehow they had made it inside her house and closed the door behind them and that was a good thing. Having an X-rated kiss on her doorstep would definitely have given her neighbors something to talk about for years.

She gazed up at him and he thought at that moment she was the most beautiful person he had ever seen. No other women he'd messed around with before could claim that. He inwardly flinched when he thought of what he'd just done. He had compared her with all the other women in his womanizing life and in essence none could compare to her. In fact, her biggest beef about having an affair with him were those other women in his life. But he knew at that moment he would give them all up for her.

The reality of him willingly doing that hit him below the belt and he nearly tumbled over. Derringer Westmoreland would give up his lifestyle for a woman?

Make a commitment to be only with her? He drew in a sharp breath. He'd never made such an allegiance with any female. Had never intended to be dedicated or devoted to one. There were too many out there and he enjoyed being footloose and fancy-free. Was she worth all of that? He knew in that instant that she was.

"What are you doing here, Derringer?"

He could tell she had regained control of the senses they'd both lost when she had opened her door. He had initiated the kiss, but she had reciprocated, which told him that although she wished otherwise, she had enjoyed it as much as he had.

"I needed to see you," he said simply.

She rolled her eyes. "That's what you said the last time."

"And I'm saying it again."

She drew in a deep breath and then turned and walked toward the sofa. He followed, thinking at least she hadn't asked him to leave…yet. She sat down on the couch and he dropped down on the love seat.

"If you had to venture out in this blasted weather, why not go visit Ashira Lattimore? I'm sure she has a bed warming for you."

The last thing he needed to do was to admit there was a strong possibility the woman did. As far as he knew, Ashira had gotten it into her head that she would eventually become Mrs. Derringer Westmoreland. He wouldn't marry Ashira if she was the last woman on earth. She was too possessive and clingy. On the other hand, the woman sitting across from him wasn't possessive and clingy enough. Yet she claimed to love him, when he knew all Ashira wanted was the Westmoreland name and all his worldly possessions.

"She isn't the woman I want warming a bed for me," he said quietly, glancing over at her intently. Not only did she look good as usual, she smelled good, too. He was so familiar with her scent that he could probably pick her out of any room even if he was blindfolded.

"Do most men care what woman warms their bed?"

He'd never cared until now.

"Don't answer, Derringer, you might incriminate yourself," she said bitterly.

That should have gotten him off the hook, but he felt a need to respond anyway. "Those who find the woman they want care. Then they are willing to give up all the others."

She lifted a brow and he knew the moment she thought she had boxed him into the perfect corner, one she figured he wouldn't be able to get out of because there was no way he would give up his other women for her. It amazed him that he could discern just how his woman thought.

His woman?

He smiled thinking that yes, she was definitely *his* woman.

"And you want me to believe you're willing to give up all other women for me," she said, chuckling with a look on her face that said the whole idea of him doing such a thing was simply ridiculous.

"Yes, I'd give up all other women for you," he said, meeting her gaze with a look that told her he was dead serious. She almost dropped the cup she was holding in her hand.

She shook her head. "Don't be silly."

"I'm not," he responded. "I'm as serious as a Bugatti Veyron on an open road."

"No, you're not."

"Oh, yes, sweetheart, I am."

She simply stared at him for a moment and then asked in a cautious and quiet tone, "Why?"

"Because you are the only woman I want," he said.

"But love has nothing to do with it?"

He knew he had to be completely honest with her. He didn't want to give her false hope or misguided illusions. "No. Love has nothing to do with it. But we'll have something just as important."

"What?"

"Respect for each other and a sense of caring. I do care for you, Lucia, or I wouldn't be here." There. He'd painted her the picture he intended for her to see. She loved him and had admitted to doing so and he had no reason not to believe her. But he knew a woman's love went deep and things could get rather messy if she expected or anticipated those feelings in return. She wouldn't get them.

"Are you willing to accept being the only woman in my life in a long-term exclusive affair, Lucia?"

She stared at him, not saying anything and then as if to be certain she'd heard him correctly and clearly understood the perimeters of what he'd proposed, she asked, "And during that time you won't be involved with any woman but me?"

"Yes, I give you my word on it. Something I've never given any woman I've been involved with in the past.

You are the first woman." It was on the tip of his lips to add, *Just like I was your first man.*

Lucia sat there, staring at Derringer and searching his face for any signs that he was being anything but aboveboard. Was he giving her a line? She drew in a deep breath. He had given her his word, and most people knew that the Westmorelands' word meant everything to them. But could it withstand temptation? What if he got tired of her and was tempted to test the waters elsewhere with someone else?

"And if you change your mind about this exclusivity thing, you will let me know? I wouldn't find out from others?"

He shook his head. "No, you wouldn't find out from others. I wouldn't do you that way, Lucia. If and when I get ready to end things between us, you will be the first to know."

He paused for a moment and then inclined his head. "So, if you fully accept those terms, please come over here for a second," he murmured in seductive invitation.

She hesitated, still uncertain. She knew there was sexual chemistry between them, she could feel the snap, crackle and pop even now with the distance separating them. On what was probably the coldest day in Denver this year, he was sitting over there looking hotter than any man had a right to look, and he got finer and finer each time she saw him. His dark eyes were pulling her in, mesmerizing her down to her panties. And that luscious mouth of his seemed to be calling out to her, tempting her in ways she really didn't need to be tempted; especially when she went to bed each night dreaming of him.

She would be the first to say that his offer of an exclusive affair surprised her because she knew that's not how he operated. In fact, that was not how any of the single Westmorelands handled their business with women. So why was he treading off the beaten track?

One thing was for certain; his blatant honesty about the kind of relationship he wanted with her had caught her off guard. He wasn't promising love, although he was well aware of how she felt about him. Instead of offering her love in return, he was offering her an exclusive affair.

Suddenly something happened that she hoped she didn't live to regret. At that moment, she began listening to her heart and not her mind. Her heart was telling her that she loved him too much not to take him up on the offer he'd laid out to her. She would be entering the affair with both eyes open and no expectations except one. He would give her advance notice when he was ready to end things between them.

That meant that while things lasted she would spend all the time with him she desired. She would be the only woman sharing his bed. The one and only woman claiming Derringer Westmoreland's full attention. She glanced down at her hand and accepted the fact that the only drawback was that he would never put a ring on her finger.

She glanced back up and her gaze returned to the deep, dark eyes that were staring at her. And waiting. And as she returned his stare, she was getting wet just thinking about all the things they would probably spend their time doing together as an exclusive couple.

She moistened her lips with the tip of her tongue and watched his gaze take in her every movement as she slowly stood. And then he stood and at that moment she realized what he was doing. Something she hadn't expected. He was meeting her halfway.

He began walking toward her the moment she began walking toward him and they met in the center. "I wasn't sure you were going to take those steps," he whispered throatily when they stood face-to-face, his mesmerizing dark gaze locked on hers.

"I wasn't sure either."

He then cupped her face in his hands and took possession of her mouth in the way she'd gotten used to him doing.

When Lucia began responding to his kiss that had liquid heat flaming inside him, he knew what they both wanted and needed. And this was the perfect day for it. He broke off the kiss and swept her off her feet and into his arms and purposefully moved toward her bedroom. Wanting her this much was the epitome of insanity, but he might as well get used to it.

He placed her on the bed and stepped back to quickly remove his clothes, sending them flying all over the place. And then for the first time since they'd made love, he took the time to use a condom.

When he returned to the bed, he captured her hand and drew her toward him to remove her clothes, slowly stripping her bare. Today she was wearing a pair of white panties, but they weren't of the granny style. They were bikinis. But the style or color of her undergarments didn't matter to him.

"Nice panties," he said, picking up his jeans and placing the panties in the back pocket.

"Why are you doing that? You have two pairs of mine already. Is there something I should know?" she asked when he tossed his jeans back to the floor and eased down onto the bed to join her.

"Yes," he said, pulling her into his arms. "I go to sleep every night with them under my pillow."

Her mouth dropped. "You're kidding, right?"

He smiled. "No, I'm not kidding, and before you ask, the answer is no. I've never collected the underwear of other women, Lucia. Just yours."

He saw the confused look on her face and thought she could dwell on what he'd confessed at another time. He needed her full concentration for what he intended to do to her right now.

Now that she was his, he wanted to get to know each and every inch of her body. Reaching out, he cradled her chin in his hand, forcing her to meet his gaze again. He could tell she was still trying to understand what he'd said earlier about her panties.

He smiled, thinking this was where he needed to shift her focus.

Lucia saw the sexy-curvy smile that touched Derringer's lips and knew she was in trouble in the most sensual way. For some reason, she knew this lovemaking session would be different, but she didn't know in what way.

"We're staying in all weekend," he whispered in a

voice so low and hot that a burning sensation began at the tips of her toes and moved upward through her body.

She was trying to understand what he'd said about staying in all weekend. Was he letting her know that he intended to keep her here, in this bed, the majority of the time? Before she could think further about it, he lifted his hand and went straight to her breasts and his fingers began toying with a darkened nipple.

"I like your breasts. I especially like how well defined they are and how easy they can slip into my mouth. Like this."

He lowered his head and his stiffened tongue laved the nipple, licking all around it a few times before easing the firm pebble between his lips, and began sucking.

Her eyes fluttered closed as a multitude of sensations pulled at the juncture of her thighs in response to the pulling motion to her breasts. His mouth was like a vacuum, drawing her nipple more and more into his mouth as his hot tongue did all kinds of wicked things to it. He switched breasts, to take on nipple number two, and she watched through hooded eyes as he continued to devour her this way.

Moments later, he drew away to lean back on his haunches to look down at her with a satisfied smile on his lips. It was then that she sensed a need in him, and the thought of him wanting her that much sent a rush of excitement through her bloodstream.

"Now for your pillows," he said, reaching behind her and grabbing both to place under her hips. She didn't have to ask what he was about to do and groaned softly at the vision that flowed through her mind. When he'd gotten her in the position he wanted, with the lower part of her elevated to his liking, he just continued to gaze at that part of her.

"You're beautiful," he whispered. "All over. But especially here," he said, reaching out and gently tracing a hand inside her inner thigh, slowly letting his fingers work their way toward the feminine folds that she knew were wet and ready for his touch.

She couldn't help but respond, and moaned as his fingers continued to lightly skim over her most intimate parts, causing sensuous shivers to flow through her. By the time he inserted two fingers inside her, she let out a deep groan and threw her head back, unable to help the way her hips rolled against the pillows cushioning them. And when he lowered his head, her fingers sank into the blades of his shoulders.

"Scent is closely linked to taste," he whispered, his breath hot against her womanly folds. "You're so wet here," he said softly, and proceeded to blow air through his lips onto her. "Since I can't blow you dry, that means I'm going to have to lap you up."

His words turned every cell in her body into a wild, unrestrained state. Instinctively, she bucked wildly against his mouth and he retaliated by grabbing her hips and diving his tongue between her womanly folds.

"Derringer!"

Her hands left his shoulders to grab hold of his head. Not to push him away, but to keep him there. Right there at that perfect angle, that most sensuous position as his mouth devoured her as if she were the tastiest meal he'd ever consumed.

She continued to cry out his name over and over,

but there was no stopping him. He used his mouth to brand the woman he wanted. And the mere thought that that woman was her made her become more and more deeply entranced with every stroke of his tongue.

And when she couldn't take any more and her body began shuddering violently in the wake of one gigantic orgasm, he wouldn't let up, but continued to make love to her this way until the last jolt passed through her body. It was then that he quickly removed the pillows from beneath her body before mounting her.

"Lucia."

Her name was a whispered hunger from Derringer's lips. Hunger that had only slightly been appeased. And when she opened glazed eyes to look up at him the exact moment he slid into her, his nostrils flared and he felt his shaft thicken even more inside her. He knew she felt it the moment that it did.

"Take me, baby, hold me, clench me. Get everything out of me that you want," he prodded in a deep, guttural voice.

And from the way her inner muscles began clenching him, clamping down tight, compressing him, he could only throw his head back, knowing he was about to enjoy the ride of his life. This was one mating he would never forget.

He began moving, thrusting in and out of her, and when she began moving in rhythm with him, the sound of flesh smacking against flesh, he let out a ragged groan. And when she locked her legs around him and rubbed her breasts against his chest, he leaned close to her mouth and captured her lips with his.

There was nothing like kissing a woman while you made love to her, he thought. Knowing your body was planted deep in hers, knowing sensual aches were being satisfied and an earth-shattering climax was on the horizon. And when she moaned deep within his mouth, he pulled back, looked down at her, wanting to see the exact moment an orgasm ripped through her.

He watched in breathless fascination as the pleasure he was giving her contorted her features, made her tremble, almost took her breath away. It was then that he felt his own body explode, and he thrust into her deeper than he'd ever gone before.

"Lucia!"

No woman had ever done this to him; reduce him to a ball of fiery sensations that had him bucking wildly all over the place. He gripped her hips as sensations continued to tear into him, enthrall him, and each desperate thrust only called for another.

And when she came again, he was right there with her and together their bodies quaked violently as unrestrained pleasure took them over the edge.

"How are we going to explain things to your family, Derringer?"

His eyes popped open and he shifted his gaze to look over at Lucia. They had taken a nap after their last lovemaking session and she was leaning down over him, still naked and with strands of her hair hanging in arousing disarray around her shoulders. He glanced beyond her to the window to look outside. Was it getting dark already? He hadn't eaten breakfast or lunch yet.

"Derringer?"

His gaze returned to her and he saw the anxiety in her eyes and the way she was nervously biting her lower lip. "We don't owe them any explanations, Lucia. We're adults."

"I know that, but…"

When she didn't complete what she was going to say, he decided to finish it off for her. "But they're going to think you've lost your mind for getting involved with me."

He knew it was true and really didn't like the way it sounded. His family knew of his reputation more than anyone, and for him to have talked Lucia into an affair wouldn't sit too well with them. But as he'd told her, he and Lucia were adults.

"They're going to think you'll eventually hurt me," she said quietly.

"Then I guess it will be on me to prove otherwise, because I'm not letting what they think cause a rift between us. Besides, they know we've been out a couple of times, and once they see how taken I am with you, they'll start minding their own business."

And he *was* taken with her, he'd admit that much. He was taken with her in a way no other woman could claim. He couldn't help but smile when he then said, "But I'm not the one they need to be concerned about. Zane's and Canyon's womanizing ways are probably right up there with Raphel's."

"Your great-grandfather? The one who was married to all those women?" she asked.

"Well, we're still trying to figure out what's fact and what's fiction. So far, the women we thought were his first two wives actually weren't. Dillon gave all the records he'd accumulated to Megan. She's determined to find out the truth as to whether Raphel actually lived all those lives," he said, pulling her down to him before he would be tempted to take one of her nipples into his mouth. As much as he loved tasting her, he figured they needed to eat something more nourishing now.

"I think I'll shower and then go into your kitchen to see what I can throw together for us," he said.

She looked surprised. "You're going to feed me?"

He couldn't help but smile, thinking that wasn't all he intended to do to her. "Yes, but trust me, I have a reason for doing so. I meant what I said earlier about keeping you inside all weekend, sweetheart."

And then he leaned down and locked his mouth with hers. This was one snowstorm that he would never forget.

Eleven

"So how are things going with you and Derringer?"

Sensations of excitement rippled in Lucia's stomach at the mention of Derringer's name. She and Chloe had decided to do lunch at McKay's, and as soon as the waitress had taken their orders and moved away, Chloe had begun asking Lucia a number of questions.

The weather had started clearing up a little on Sunday night, and Derringer had talked her into going to his ranch and leaving for work on Monday morning from there. He had even helped her pack an overnight bag. What she hadn't expected was his siblings and cousins showing up early Monday morning to check on him because no one had seen or heard from him all weekend. She hadn't missed the look of surprise on their faces when she'd come down the stairs dressed for work, giving everyone a clear idea of how he'd spent those snowed-in hours and with whom.

That had been a couple of weeks ago. "So far, so good. I enjoy spending time with him."

And truly she did. He'd taken her to the movies several times and picked her up from work on several occasions, and had spent the night over at her place a number of times as well.

Chloe beamed. "I'm glad. Ramsey is too. Already he's seen a change in Derringer."

Lucia raised a brow as she took a sip of her iced tea. "What kind of change?"

"Peace. Calm. He seems more focused. Less untamed and wild. Not only Ramsey but the other Westmorelands think you're good for him."

Lucia nervously nibbled at her lower lip. "I hope they aren't getting any ideas. I told you what's between me and Derringer is only temporary. He made sure I understood that, Chloe."

Chloe waved her words away. "All men think nothing is forever at first, only a few have love on their minds initially. Callum was an exception. He knew he loved Gemma before she had a clue."

"But Derringer doesn't love me. He's said as much. I'm in this relationship with both eyes open."

Later, back in her office, she recalled her words to Chloe as she sat staring at the huge arrangement of flowers that was sitting on her desk that had been delivered while she was at lunch. The card had simply said, *I'm thinking of you.*

Just the thought that he was thinking of her made everything inside her rock with anticipation to see him again. It was Friday and they were going skating again tonight and she couldn't wait.

The intercom on her desk went off, almost startling her. "Yes?"

"Someone is here to see you, Ms. Conyers."

Excitement flowed in her stomach. The last time she'd received flowers from Derringer, he had shown up at her office later. Was he here to see her now? "Who is it, Wanda?"

"Ashira Lattimore."

Lucia's throat tightened. Why would Ashira Lattimore be visiting her? There was only one way to find out. "Thanks, Wanda, ask her to come in."

Lucia clicked off her intercom and glanced at the flowers on her desk. Something about them gave her inner strength to deal with what was about to take place. She wasn't exactly sure what would happen, but she figured it had something to do with Derringer.

It wasn't long before the woman knocked on her door. "Come in."

Ashira walked in and just like all the other times Lucia had seen her she looked beautiful. But Lucia knew that beauty was merely on the outside. She had heard a number of stories about the spoiled and reckless woman who had long ago stamped ownership on Derringer. In a way she was surprised Ashira hadn't confronted her before now.

"Ashira, this is a surprise. What can *Simply Irresistible* do for you?" Lucia plastered a smile on her lips.

The woman didn't bother returning her fabricated smile. "I've been gone, Lucia, visiting a sick relative in Dakota, and thought I'd let you know I'm back."

Lucia placed her arms across her chest. "And that's supposed to mean something to me?"

The woman glanced at the flowers on Lucia's desk, paused a minute and then said, "I think it would where Derringer is concerned. Not sure if he told you, but the two of us have an understanding."

"Do you?"

"Yes. No matter who he dallies with, I'm the one he'll always come back to. I'm sure you've known him long enough to know our history."

"Unfortunately, I don't, and for you to pay me a visit to stake a claim you think you have speaks volumes. It makes me think you're not as confident as you want to claim," she said with more bravado than she actually felt.

"Think whatever you want. Just remember, when he's done with you he'll come back to me. He and I have plans to marry one day."

Lucia's heart dropped at the woman's announcement. "Congratulations on your and Derringer's future plans. Now, if you've said everything you've come here to say, I think you should leave."

It was then that Ashira smiled, but the smile didn't quite reach her eyes. It didn't come close. "Fine, just remember my warning. I'm trying to spare you any heartbreak." The woman then walked out of her office.

Derringer's gaze flickered over Lucia's face. "You okay? You've been quiet most of the evening."

They had gone skating with what he was now beginning to think of as the regular crowd. Most of the kids and teens had gotten used to him and Lucia invading their turf. And now they were back at her place, but she hadn't said a whole lot since he'd picked her up that evening.

She smiled over at him. "Yes, I'm fine. This has been a busy week at work and I'm just glad it's the weekend. I need it."

He pulled her into his arms. "And I need it as well. More horses are arriving this week and then all our relatives start arriving the week after that for the Westmoreland Charity Ball. You are going to the ball with me, aren't you?"

He watched her features and she seemed surprised he'd asked. Her next question proved him right. "You really want to take me?"

"Of course I do."

"Thanks."

He stared down at her for a moment. "Why are you thanking me?"

"Um, no reason. I just wasn't sure what your plans would be."

It was on the tip of his tongue to say that whatever his plans were they would always include her, but he didn't. Lately, he was encountering feelings and emotions when it came to Lucia that he didn't quite understand and didn't want to dwell on.

"I hear Gemma is coming home in a few days," she said, cutting into his thoughts.

A smile touched his lips. "Yeah, and I miss her. I'd gotten used to Gemma being underfoot and wasn't sure how I'd handle her up and moving to Australia. But

Callum loves her and we know he's taking good care of her. Besides, homecomings are good."

"Yes, he does love her."

There was something about her tone of voice that sounded contemplative and reflective, as if she was wondering, considering just how that would be for a man to love her that way. For a moment he didn't know what to say, so he decided not to say anything.

Instead, he did something he always enjoyed doing to her. He touched her chin, making rotary motions with his thumb on her soft skin before tilting her head back to lower his mouth to kiss her.

The sound of her sensual purr fueled his desire, making him so aroused his erection thickened painfully against the zipper of his jeans. And when she wrapped her arms around his neck as he deepened the kiss, he went crazy with lust for her.

Not able to hold back any longer, he swept her off her feet into his arms and carried her upstairs to the bedroom.

"Why haven't you mentioned Ashira's visit to Derringer, Lucia?"

Lucia glanced over at Chloe. They had just finished a business meeting and she'd known something had been on her best friend's mind all morning. "And how do you know I haven't?"

"Trust me, had you told him, all hell would have broken loose. He's never appreciated Ashira's possessiveness."

Lucia shrugged. "For all I know they could have an understanding just like she claims."

"I can't believe you would think that."

"In all honesty I'm trying not to think about anything regarding Derringer and Ashira. I'm just taking one day at a time."

Chloe frowned. "She would never have come into *my* office with that haughty I'm-Derringer's-real-woman foolishness, trust me."

"Because you know Ramsey loves you, I can't say that for Derringer and me. I know he doesn't love me," she said softly.

Later that night she lay in Derringer's arms with her naked body spooned intimately to his. His arm was thrown over her and he slept with his hand cupping her breast. His warm body and the scent of his musky masculinity surrounded her and she became aroused by it. That was something she couldn't help.

Since becoming sexually involved with Derringer, she had become more aware of herself as a woman, particularly her needs and wants, mainly because he made her feel as if she was the most enticing and alluring woman he'd ever met. And coming from a man like Derringer, that meant a lot.

She then thought about her conversation with Chloe earlier that day. Maybe she should have mentioned Ashira's visit to her office to Derringer. And yet a part of her didn't want to draw him into any women-over-man drama. Besides, time would tell if what the woman said was true.

She knew the moment he'd awakened by the change in his breathing. The other telltale sign was the feel of his erection beginning to swell against her naked backside. And then he began touching her. With the hand that wasn't cupping her breast he started at the dip in her thigh and let his fingers do a little walking, tracing a line toward her waist. It then followed the curve toward the juncture at her inner thighs.

"Shift open your legs for me, baby," he leaned over to whisper in her ear. "I need to touch you there."

She did what he asked and moments later she was moaning at his exploratory touch. And then when the hand cupping her breasts began doing its own thing by torturing her nipples, she clenched her lips to keep from crying out his name.

"You're so passionate," he murmured close to her ear. "You are the most sensuous woman I know."

She wanted so much to believe him. She wanted to believe it was her that he wanted and not Ashira. And when she couldn't take his torture any longer, she cried out for him to make love to her.

"My pleasure."

He then eased her onto her back and straddled her, and before she could draw her next breath, he entered her, melding their bodies as one. And each time he stroked into her and retreated, she ground her body against him ready for his reentry.

Over and over, back and forth, performing the mating dance the two of them had created as he thrust in and out of her and all she could do was continue to groan out her cries of pleasure. And when a guttural moan flowed from Derringer's lips, she knew they had been tossed into the turbulent waves of pure ecstasy.

Incredible.

Derringer pulled in a deep breath. That's how he

always thought of making love with Lucia. Each and every time was simply incredible. And she was incredible. He glanced over at her and saw she had fallen asleep with her body spooned against his.

The room was quiet as images flickered in his mind of all the things they'd done together over the past few weeks, and not all of them had been in the bedroom. He enjoyed taking her places, being seen with her and spending time with her. Exclusivity was working, but he knew it was only because the woman was Lucia.

No other woman crossed his mind. He didn't want any other woman but her. And his inner fear of something happening to her lessened more and more each day. When he considered all the possibilities, weighed all his options and thought of what could happen, none of it was more significant than spending time with her, being with her. For the rest of his life. He loved her.

Derringer drew in a sharp breath because at that moment he couldn't imagine being without her…. He wanted to live each day to the fullest with her, loving her completely. She was the only woman he wanted. For his soul mate and then one day for his wife.

His wife.

A smile touched his lips. No other woman deserved that title. And he was determined that Lucia—only Lucia—would wear it. He knew he couldn't rush her. He had to take things slow and believe that one day she would realize she was the only woman who could be a wife for this Westmoreland.

The following days passed quickly and everyone was excited when Gemma returned home and confirmed the rumor that she and Callum would become parents in seven months. It was decided that a cookout was in order to welcome the couple home and to celebrate their good news. Another Westmoreland baby was on the way.

Derringer, his brothers and cousins were playing a friendly game of horseshoes when someone rang the bell letting them know it was time to eat. The men went into Dillon's kitchen to wash up, when Zane leaned over and whispered, "Lucia looks just like she belongs with the Westmorelands, Derringer."

His gaze moved across the yard to where she was helping Chloe and Megan set the table. Zane was right. She did look as if she belonged, mainly because she did belong. In a way, he'd always known that. And now he was waiting patiently for her to realize it as well.

They had been spending a lot of time together lately. It had become his regular routine to go home and shower after working with the horses and then head on over to her place each day. School was out, so she was home most evenings now. They cooked dinner together, on occasion they would go out to take in a movie or shoot pool—something he had shown her how to do. Then on Friday nights they went roller skating. But he also enjoyed those times they would stay inside to cuddle on the sofa and watch videos.

As if she felt him looking at her, she glanced over at him and an intimate connection, as well as sexual chemistry, flowed between them the way it always did. A slow, flirty smile touched his lips and he tipped his hat to her. She returned his smile and nodded before returning to what she was doing.

"I think you like her," Zane said, reminding Derringer he was there.

Derringer smiled at his brother, refusing to let Zane bait him. "Of course I like her. We all do."

"Hey, don't be an ass, Derringer. You're in love with the woman. Admit it."

Derringer only smiled and glanced back to where Lucia was sitting. The women were crowded together on the porch listening to Gemma share stories about her Australian adventure and how she was settling into her role as Mrs. Callum Austell.

He couldn't help it, but he kept looking at Lucia. Each and every time he saw her, spent time with her, he fell more and more in love with her. Now he understood how Dillon could have left home to investigate all the rumors they'd heard about Raphel and return less than a month later an engaged man. At first he thought his cousin had needed to have his head examined, but once he met Pam and had seen how Dillon would light up around her, he sort of understood. But he'd figured nothing like that would ever happen to him.

He had been proven wrong.

He loved everything about Lucia, including her interaction with his family. But mainly he loved the way she made him feel whenever they were together.

His thoughts were pulled back to the present when Jason took a minute to provide an update on old man's Bostwick's granddaughter from Savannah. Folks were saying the woman was supposed to arrive in town to claim her inheritance in a couple of weeks. Jason was anxious about that and he was hoping his offer for the land and Hercules was the one the woman would accept.

"Looks like we have a visitor," Canyon whispered. "At least, she's *your* visitor, Derringer."

Derringer frowned when he saw the sports car driven by Ashira Lattimore pull up in the yard. He couldn't help wondering what she wanted since he knew she hadn't been invited. Also, Ashira and his sisters didn't get along. But that had never stopped Ashira from thinking her lack of an invite was merely an oversight on someone's part. She was her parents' only child and was spoiled rotten. In contrast, he thought, Lucia was her parents' only child, yet she was sweet as wine. The difference in the two women was like night and day.

"Hello, everyone," she called out, waving, while glancing around as if she had every right to show up at a family function uninvited. Her face lit up in a huge smile when she saw Derringer, and she immediately headed toward him.

"Derringer, sweetheart, I've missed you." She leaned over, wrapped her arms around his neck and placed a kiss on his lips in full view of everyone.

He took her arms from around his neck and stared down at her. "What are you doing here, Ashira?"

She gave him a pouty look. "I came to see you."

"This is not where I live," he said in an annoyed voice.

"I know, but you weren't home and we need to talk."

"About what?"

She leaned up on tiptoe and whispered close to his ear, "About that horse you're trying to sell Daddy. Since he's buying it for me, I think we need to discuss it, don't you?"

"I'm busy right now, Ashira."

"But you want to make that sale, don't you? Daddy is ready. He wants to see you now, at the ranch."

Derringer knew he needed to put Ashira in her place once and for all, but here was not the place to do it. "Okay, let's go," he said, gripping her hand and pulling her with him toward her car. "I'll be back later," he called over his shoulder to everyone. "I've got some business to take care of."

He was angry. He didn't care about the horse sale as much as Ashira assumed that he did. If she thought it was a carrot she could dangle in front of him to make him do what she wanted then she had another thought coming. What ticked him off more than anything was her underhanded behavior. He should have put her in her place regarding him years ago.

He was so intent on taking her off somewhere to give her a piece of his mind, that he didn't notice the haughty look of victory the woman shot over her shoulder at Lucia.

Chloe drew in a deep breath. "I don't think you should leave, Lucia."

Lucia wiped the tears from her eyes. "There's no reason for me to stay," she said, gathering up her things. "You saw it for yourself. Ashira shows up and he leaves. She wanted to prove what she told me that day was true and she did."

Chloe shook her head. "But I don't think that's the way it was. According to Zane and Jason, Derringer

said it was about business and probably had to talk to
her about that horse he's trying to sell her father."

"And it couldn't wait? Please don't make excuses for
what I saw with my own eyes, Chloe. She snaps her
finger and he takes off. He was leading her over to the
car and not the other way around. And I truly don't want
to be here when they come back."

She reached out and hugged Chloe and whispered in
a broken voice, "I'll call you later."

Lucia knew it would be hard telling the others
goodbye. They would see the hurt in her eyes and they
would pity her. Or it might be one of those you-should-
have-known-better-than-to-fall-in-love-with-Derringer
looks. In her book, one was just as bad as the other.

Somehow she made it through, but nearly broke when
Zane pulled her into his arms and asked her to stay a
while longer. She forced a smile up at him and told him
she couldn't, before rushing to her car, getting inside
and driving away.

Derringer returned over an hour later. He hadn't
meant to be gone that long, but when he'd arrived at
the Lattimores' place he had encountered more drama.
Ashira had given her father the impression things were
serious between them and he had to first break the
news to Phillip Lattimore that they weren't. And then
he had to let Ashira know that he didn't consider her a
candidate as a wife, at least not for him since there was
no way in hell he would ever get shackled with someone
as spoiled and selfish as she was. Those words hadn't
been too well received, and Derringer had found himself

stranded on the Lattimore land. He'd had to call Pete to give him a lift back here.

The moment he got out of Pete's patrol car he knew something was wrong. He could understand everyone staring at him, probably wondering why Pete, instead of Ashira, had brought him back. But they weren't just staring at him. They were openly glaring.

"Looks like your family is pissed off at you for some reason," Pete said.

"Yes, looks that way," he responded. "Thanks for bringing me here."

Once the patrol car had driven off, Derringer's gaze roamed over the group that were outside in the yard cleaning up from today's activities. He looked for one person in particular, but he didn't see her. "Where's Lucia?"

It was Canyon who answered in a belligerent tone, "Oh, so now you remember that she does exist?"

Derringer frowned. "What are you talking about?"

Dillon folded his arms over his chest. "You invited Lucia here, yet you took off with another woman without giving her a backward glance. I expected better of you, Derringer."

Derringer's frown deepened. "That's not the way it was."

It was Ramsey who spoke up. "That's the way we saw it."

"And that's the way Lucia saw it," Bailey snapped, losing her cool. "I can't believe you would leave here with one of those 'silly' girls—in fact, the silliest of them all—deserting Lucia and then showing back up an hour later expecting her to still be here waiting on you. You are so full of yourself."

"Like I said, that's not the way it was," he said, glancing around at all his family circling around him.

"You're going to have a hard time convincing Lucia of that," Chloe said, not with the same snappish tone Bailey had used, but there was no doubt in everyone's mind that if given the chance she would clobber this particular brother-in-law right about now.

"Especially when just a couple of weeks ago Ashira paid Lucia a visit at *Simply Irresistible* and warned her that she could get you back anytime she wanted, and that the two of you have an understanding and that she would be the one who would eventually become your wife," Chloe added in disgust.

"Like hell," Derringer snarled.

"Doesn't matter. Ashira came here today to prove a point and in Lucia's eyes, she did."

"But like I said, it wasn't that way," Derringer implored. He then outlined everything that had happened once he'd left with Ashira and the reason that he'd left with her in the first place. "And I won't let that sort of misunderstanding come between me and Lucia," he said, moving toward his truck. "I need to go see her."

She wasn't home when Derringer got there, but according to her neighbor, Mrs. Noel, she had been there, rushing in and then leaving with an overnight bag. Derringer had no idea where she had gone. And she wouldn't answer her cell phone, although he had left several messages for her. He knew her parents were still in Tennessee and wouldn't be returning for another week or so. Thinking she'd possibly driven out to their place to stay for the night, he had gone there too, only to find the Conyers's homestead deserted.

It was after midnight when he returned to his place and rushed over to his phone when it began ringing the moment he opened the door. "Hello?"

"This is Chloe. I just got a call from Lucia. She's fine and asked that you not try seeing her or calling her. She needs time."

"No, she needs me just like I need her. She should have told me about Ashira's visit and I would have straightened things out then. I need to talk with her, Chloe. I can't stand to lose her."

"And why can't you stand to lose her, Derringer? What makes her so different from the others?"

He knew why Chloe was goading him. He was well aware what she was trying to get him to admit, not only to himself, but to her as well, just how he felt about Lucia. "I love her." He drew in a deep breath. "I love her so damn much."

"Then somehow you're going to have to convince her of that, not only in words, but with actions. Good night, Derringer."

Chloe then hung up the phone.

Twelve

Lucia sat behind her desk and stared at the beautiful arrangement of flowers that had arrived that morning. She then glanced around her office at the others that had arrived during the week. The cards all said the same thing: *You are the only woman I want.*

She drew in a deep breath wishing she could believe that, but for some reason she couldn't. Maybe it had to do with the haughty I-told-you-so look Ashira had had on her face when she had left that day with Derringer. The two of them had a history. The woman had been after Derringer for years and it seemed as if she had him. And according to Ashira, no matter who he messed around with, *she* would be the woman he married.

So, Lucia couldn't help asking herself, why was she wasting her time and her heart? The latter she knew there was no answer for. She would continue to love him, no matter what. Always had and always would. But she could do something about the former. To spend any more time with him was heartbreak just waiting to happen. Of course, he wouldn't see it that way. Men had a tendency to look at affairs differently. They didn't have a clue when it came to emotions.

At least he was respecting her wishes and hadn't tried contacting her again. She figured he and Ashira were now a hot item, although Chloe insisted otherwise. Of course, she had come up with an excuse for the reason he'd left, which Lucia was certain was the one he'd told everyone. Little did he know that Ashira was spreading another story. She wanted to make sure word got back to Lucia through mutual acquaintances that she and Derringer had left the party to go to his place and have hot, blazing sex. It deeply pained Lucia that he could leave her bed that morning and hop into bed with another woman less than twelve hours later.

Lucia glanced up when she heard the knock at her office door. "Come in."

Chloe stuck her head in and smiled. "Word is around the office that you got more flowers."

She came in and closed the door behind her, admiring the arrangement sitting on Lucia's desk. "They are gorgeous, but then, all the bouquets Derringer has sent have been gorgeous. You have to admit that."

Lucia smiled slowly. "Yes, they've all been gorgeous, but they don't mean a thing."

Chloe took the chair across from her desk. "Because of what Tanya McCoy called and told you yesterday? That she'd heard Ashira and Derringer left my place and had hot, rousing sex over at Derringer's Dungeon?

I don't believe that and neither should you. Ashira is just trying to save face. I was there when Derringer returned in Pete's patrol car. Don't let Ashira continue to mess with your mind like that. You need to take Derringer's message on those cards you've been getting with the flowers to heart."

Lucia fought back tears. "I wish I could, but I can't. All these years I've loved him and was fine with loving him from a distance. But then I had to go ruin everything by admitting I loved him and letting him into my space. From now on it's going back to status quo."

"Does that mean you won't ever visit your god-daughter at my place, for fear of running into Derringer?"

"No, but I'm trying to get beyond that."

"Then I think this coming Saturday is the perfect way to start. I suggest you change your mind about coming to the Westmoreland Charity Ball. If you see Derringer, no big deal. Now is your time to show him once and for all that you've gotten over him and you're moving on and won't be hiding out to avoid him."

Lucia nervously nibbled on her bottom lip. "And what if he's there with Ashira?"

"And what if he is? It's his loss. And if he wants her instead of you then more power to him. But if I were you, I would definitely let him see what he gave up. Um, I think you and I should go shopping."

Lucia wasn't convinced making an appearance at the charity ball this weekend would be the right thing to do.

"Just because you think one Westmoreland acted like

an ass is no reason to ostracize yourself from the rest of us," Chloe added.

Lucia knew what Chloe just said was true. Gemma had called her this morning and she had yet to call her back. So had Megan and Bailey earlier in the week. They had been friends long before she'd met Derringer. It wasn't their fault that she had fallen head over heels in love with their brother, a man who would never settle down, fall in love and marry any woman. Except maybe Ashira one day when he got tired of playing the field.

She tossed her pen on the desk and met Chloe's gaze. "Maybe you're right. I can't avoid the other Westmorelands just because my affair with Derringer went sour."

A smile touched Chloe's lips. "No, you can't. So are we going shopping this weekend?"

Lucia chuckled. "Yes, and I know this is more about you than me, Chloe Burton Westmoreland. You'll do anything, come up with any excuse, to shop."

Chloe stood, smiling. "Hey, what can I say? A woman has to do what a woman has to do."

Derringer glanced around. He was surrounded by Westmorelands and he couldn't help but smile. Once a year all the Westmorelands—from the south and west—got together for a family reunion rotating between Atlanta, rural Montana and Denver. At other times they got together to support each other for various events. Earlier this year they had traveled to Austin to be with their cousins: Cole, Clint and Casey Westmoreland had honored their deceased uncle during the Sid Roberts Foundation annual charity ball. And usually every year there seemed to be a Westmoreland wedding. The last one had been Gemma's a few months back.

And now all the Atlanta and Montana Westmorelands were gathered here in Denver with their wives for the Westmoreland Charity Ball. They had begun arriving a few days ago and were all accounted for as of noon today when Thorn and Tara had arrived. Thorn had come straight from Bikers' Week in Myrtle Beach, South Carolina.

"Thanks for putting us up for the next couple of days, Derringer."

He glanced around and smiled at his cousins, the twins—Storm and Chase. But then there were several sets of twins in the Atlanta Westmorelands' group. Storm and Chase's father had been a twin, and his cousins, Ian and Quade, were twins as well.

"Hey, no problem. If there's anything you need, just let me know." At that moment his cell phone went off and when he saw it was Chloe he smiled. "Excuse me while I take this."

He went outside to sit on the porch. "Yes, Chloe?"

"You owe me big-time, Derringer, and I swear, if you screw up, I'm coming after you myself."

He believed her. "Trust me, I've got everything planned. I'm just grateful you got Lucia to agree to come to the charity ball."

"It wasn't easy. Ashira and her girls are out spreading lies, claiming that when you left the cookout, you took her to Derringer's Dungeon and got busy."

Derringer's mouth dropped. They hadn't gone near his home. "That's a lie."

"I know, but she's intent on spreading that rumor. I

don't know what you have planned for the ball, but it better be good, and hopefully it will put a stop to Ashira once and for all."

Derringer nodded. "Trust me. It will."

"You sure you're all right, sweetheart?"

Lucia glanced over at her parents, namely, her dad, who had a concerned look on his face. "Yes, Dad, I'm fine."

He smiled. "Well, you look simply beautiful."

And considering everything, she felt beautiful. Chloe had nearly worn her out last weekend. They hadn't just shopped in Denver but had caught one of those commuter planes to Boulder to do some shopping there as well. In the end, she felt like Cinderella entering the ball. And just like good ole Cinderella she feared she would leave the ball without her man.

The moment she and her parents entered the huge ballroom she drew in a deep breath at the number of people in attendance. But then, she really wasn't surprised. The Westmoreland Foundation provided funds to a number of charities and for that very reason the people of Denver were always supportive.

It didn't take long to pick out all the Westmorelands, especially the males. Whether they were from the north, south, east or west, they had similar looks and builds. In their black tuxes, they were all tall, dashing and ultrahandsome and, not surprisingly, even with their wives on their arms most of the other women present had their eyes on them with wishful expressions on their faces.

She had met all of them at Chloe's wedding and

again at Gemma's. They were a nice group of people and she thought Chloe was blessed to be a part of the Westmoreland clan.

It seemed Chloe spotted her the moment she arrived and eagerly pulled her from her parents' side, telling her over and over just how ravishing she looked. So did Bailey, Megan, Gemma and a number of the other Westmoreland women. All the men spoke to her and as usual Zane gave her a naughty wink, which made her chuckle.

She released a deep breath, glad no one was acting or behaving any differently toward her, although all that might change once Derringer arrived with Ashira on his arm. She was just speculating and couldn't help doing so when both he and Ashira didn't appear to be present. No sooner had that thought left her mind than she glanced up and Ashira walked in with a couple of her girlfriends. Lucia was surprised she wasn't with Derringer.

A short while later, Lucia was dancing with Jason when Derringer cut in. She glanced up and tried her best not to narrow her gaze at him. The last thing she wanted was to let him know just how badly he had hurt her, although she was sure he had a clue, which was the reason for the flowers. But if he thought he could woo her and sleep with Ashira at the same time then he had another thought coming.

"Lucia."

She wished he didn't say her name quite that way. With that same throatiness she remembered so well. "Derringer."

"You look beautiful."

"Thanks. You look handsome yourself." That was no lie. For some reason, tonight he looked more handsome than ever.

"I'm glad you came."

"Are you?"

"Yes, and I hope you liked the flowers."

"I did, but they mean nothing as far as rekindling our relationship. It's over, Derringer."

He shook his head. "Things will never be over between us. If you read all those cards then you know you're the only woman I want."

She rolled her eyes. "Yeah, right, go tell that to someone else."

He smiled. "I don't have a problem telling anyone else. In fact, I think I will tell everyone."

He turned and gave the orchestra a cue to stop playing and everything got quiet. Also, as if on cue, someone handed him a microphone. "May I have everyone's attention, please?"

Aghast, she tried tugging her hand from his. "What do you think you're doing?" She wanted to run and hide when her words got captured on the mic for all to hear. She was certain before the night was over she would die of shame.

"I'm about to speak from my heart," he said, holding tight to her hand.

"When it comes to the ladies, I didn't know you had a heart, Derringer," Pete called out.

She tried not to glance around since she knew all eyes were on them. They were in the middle of the ballroom's dance floor, and everyone, curious as to what was going on, had moved closer to watch. The

Westmorelands, she noted, were standing in a cluster behind Derringer as if to show a united front.

A smile touched Derringer's lips, but when he turned around and met her gaze, his expression got serious. Then he said in a loud and clear voice, "I didn't know I had a heart either until Lucia captured it." He paused and then added, "And that is something no other woman has been able to do."

She glanced away, refusing to believe what she thought she heard him saying. She didn't want to make a mistake about what he was saying. There was no way it could be true.

As if he'd read her thoughts, he tugged on her hand to make her look back at him. "It's true, Lucia. I am so hopelessly in love with you I can't think straight. You are so filled with goodness, warmth and love, I can't imagine not loving you. And it's not anything I discovered upon waking this morning. I knew that I loved you for a while, but didn't want to. I have this fear of loving someone and then losing that person. I think a number of us Denver Westmorelands can't help but feel that way due to the catastrophic losses we've endured in the past. It can do something to you. It can make you not want to take a chance and get attached to anyone.

"But I want to get attached to you. I have to get attached to you. You make me whole. Without you I am nothing."

Lucia couldn't stop the tears that began falling from her eyes. She couldn't believe what he was saying. Derringer was declaring his love and his need for her in front of everyone. His family. Her parents. Their neighbors and friends. Ashira. Ashira's girlfriends. Ashira's parents. Everyone who wanted to hear it.

Evidently, Ashira and her girlfriends didn't. Lucia watched them walk out. It didn't matter to her. The man she had loved for a lifetime was letting her know in front of everyone that he loved her back.

"And when a man has that much love for any woman," Derringer was saying, bringing her attention back to him, "he will choose that woman as his mate for life. The woman he wants for his wife."

She then watched in shock as he eased down on bended knee, gripped her hand tighter and then held her gaze. "Lucia, will you marry me? Will you take my name? Have my babies? And continue to make me happy? In turn, I will be the best husband to you. I will love you. Honor you and cherish you for as long as I live. Will you marry me?"

While she was still swooning from his public proposal, she felt a ring being slid onto her finger. She glanced down. The diamond sparkled so brightly it almost blinded her. She could only stare at it in amazement.

"You have a proposal on the table, Lucia. Please answer the man," someone called out from the crowd.

She couldn't help but smile as she swiped her tears. That had been her father's voice. She met Derringer's gaze. He was still on his knees waiting. "Oh, Derringer," she said through her tears. "Yes! Yes! I will marry you!"

Smiling, he got to his feet and pulled her into his arms in a deep, passionate kiss. She was not sure how long the kiss lasted. The only thing she did know was that the orchestra was playing music again and others were dancing all around them. They didn't care. Tonight was their night and they were going to take full advantage of it.

Hours later, Derringer and Lucia lay together naked in the bed where their adventure all began at Derringer's Dungeon. Upon hearing her wake up during the night, he was ready and leaned up on his elbow and looked down at her, his gaze hot as it roamed over every inch of her naked body.

He leaned down and kissed her and moaned deep in his throat when she returned the kiss with the same hunger he was giving her. Moments later when he pulled back he could only draw in a deep breath in total amazement. Would he always want her to this extreme? He smiled, knowing that yes, he would.

"I love you," he whispered softy. "I regret all the years I didn't make you my one and only girl."

Lucia smiled up at him. "You weren't ready for that type of serious move back then, and in a way I'm glad." She chuckled. "Besides, you needed to impress my dad."

"And you think I did?"

Her smile brightened. "Yes. Going to him and asking for his permission to marry me scored you a lot of brownie points for sure. You're going to be a son-in-law for life."

"Baby, I intend to be a husband for life as well. And you will be my wife for life."

He ran his fingers through her hair as he leaned down

and captured her mouth with his. She was definitely a wife for a Westmoreland. She was his, and their love was just the beginning.

Epilogue

A month and a half later

"Okay, Derringer, you may kiss your bride."

A huge smile lit Derringer's features when he pulled Lucia into his arms. She was the woman he wanted, the wife he desired, and as he captured her mouth with his he knew they would share a long and wonderful life together.

He finally released her and turned to their guests as the minister presented them to everyone as Mr. and Mrs. Derringer Westmoreland. He loved the sound of that and wondered why he'd let his fear keep him away from the altar for so long. But as Lucia had said, he hadn't been ready until now.

A short while later, with his wife's hand tucked in his, they made their way around his property, which the women of the family had transformed from Derringer's Dungeon to Derringer and Lucia's Castle. Gemma had returned the week before the wedding and had worked alongside the wedding planner to give Lucia the wedding she deserved.

He glanced down at her and tightened her hand in his. "Happy?"

She smiled up at him. "Immensely so."

He thought she looked beautiful and doubted he would ever forget how he felt the moment he saw her walking down the aisle to him on her father's arm. She was the most beautiful vision in white that he'd ever seen. They had decided to travel to Dubai for their honeymoon, and while they were across the waters they planned to visit Callum and Gemma in Australia before returning home.

"Time for you to throw your bouquet to the single ladies, Lucia," the wedding planner came up to say.

Lucia turned to Derringer and placed a kiss on his lips. "I'll be back in a moment," she whispered.

"And I'll be right here waiting," was his response. He watched her walk to an area where over thirty women— that included his sisters—stood waiting.

"I've never seen you so happy, Derringer," Jason said, smiling as he walked up. "Congratulations."

"Thanks, and I'm going to give you the same advice I gave Zane, Riley, Canyon and Stern this morning at breakfast, although I could tell they didn't want to hear it. Being single is nice, but being married is much sweeter. Trust me, two is better than one."

Derringer figured if he could get any of his single cousins to take his advice it would be Jason. He had been standing with Jason at the charity ball the moment old man Bostwick's granddaughter had made her entrance. It had been obvious that Jason had been spellbound, entranced by the woman's beauty.

He looked over at Jason. "So, have you officially met Bostwick's granddaughter yet?"

Jason smiled. "Yes, I introduced myself at the ball. Her name is Elizabeth but she prefers being called Bella."

Derringer nodded. "Did you let her know you were interested in her land and in Hercules?"

"Yes, we spoke briefly before Kenneth Bostwick interrupted us. I hear she's trying to make up her mind about what she wants to do. I don't think she's interested in hanging around these parts. This is no place for a Southern belle and besides, she knows nothing about ranching."

"But you do. You can always show her the ropes."

Jason looked shocked at the suggestion. "Why would I want to do something like that? She has two things I want—her land and that stallion. The sooner she decides to sell and return to Savannah, the sooner I can get both. I'd do just about anything to get the land and that horse."

Derringer glanced up at Jason and saw his cousin was serious. "Just remember what I said, Jason. Worldly possessions aren't everything. The love of a good woman is."

He then watched as Lucia began walking back over toward him. She was a good woman. She was his life and now she was his wife.

* * * * *

COMING NEXT MONTH

Available May 10, 2011

You can find more information on upcoming
Harlequin® titles, free excerpts and more at
www.HarlequinInsideRomance.com.

REQUEST YOUR FREE BOOKS!
2 FREE NOVELS PLUS 2 FREE GIFTS!

Harlequin®

Desire

ALWAYS POWERFUL, PASSIONATE AND PROVOCATIVE

YES! Please send me 2 FREE Harlequin Desire® novels and my 2 FREE gifts (gifts are worth about $10). After receiving them, if I don't wish to receive any more books, I can return the shipping statement marked "cancel." If I don't cancel, I will receive 6 brand-new novels every month and be billed just $4.05 per book in the U.S. or $4.74 per book in Canada. That's a saving of at least 15% off the cover price! It's quite a bargain! Shipping and handling is just 50¢ per book in the U.S. and 75¢ per book in Canada.* I understand that accepting the 2 free books and gifts places me under no obligation to buy anything. I can always return a shipment and cancel at any time. Even if I never buy another book, the two free books and gifts are mine to keep forever.

225/326 SDN FC65

Name _____ (PLEASE PRINT) _____

Address _____ Apt. # _____

City _____ State/Prov. _____ Zip/Postal Code _____

Signature (if under 18, a parent or guardian must sign)

Mail to the **Reader Service:**

IN U.S.A.: P.O. Box 1867, Buffalo, NY 14240-1867
IN CANADA: P.O. Box 609, Fort Erie, Ontario L2A 5X3

Not valid for current subscribers to Harlequin Desire books.

Want to try two free books from another line?
Call 1-800-873-8635 or visit www.ReaderService.com.

* Terms and prices subject to change without notice. Prices do not include applicable taxes. Sales tax applicable in N.Y. Canadian residents will be charged applicable taxes. Offer not valid in Quebec. This offer is limited to one order per household. All orders subject to credit approval. Credit or debit balances in a customer's account(s) may be offset by any other outstanding balance owed by or to the customer. Please allow 4 to 6 weeks for delivery. Offer available while quantities last.

Your Privacy—The Reader Service is committed to protecting your privacy. Our Privacy Policy is available online at www.ReaderService.com or upon request from the Reader Service.

We make a portion of our mailing list available to reputable third parties that offer products we believe may interest you. If you prefer that we not exchange your name with third parties, or if you wish to clarify or modify your communication preferences, please visit us at www.ReaderService.com/consumerschoice or write to us at Reader Service Preference Service, P.O. Box 9062, Buffalo, NY 14269. Include your complete name and address.

HDES11

*With an evil force hell-bent on destruction,
two enemies must unite to find a truth that turns
all-too-personal when passions collide.*

*Enjoy a sneak peek in Jenna Kernan's next installment
in her original* TRACKER *series, GHOST STALKER,
available in May, only from Harlequin Nocturne.*

"**W**ho are you?" he snarled.

Jessie lifted her chin. "Your better."

His smile was cold. "Such arrogance could only come from a Niyanoka."

She nodded. "Why are you here?"

"I don't know." He glanced about her room. "I asked the birds to take me to a healer."

"And they have done so. Is that *all* you asked?"

"No. To lead them away from my friends." His eyes fluttered and she saw them roll over white.

Jessie straightened, preparing to flee, but he roused himself and mastered the momentary weakness. His eyes snapped open, locking on her.

Her heart hammered as she inched back.

"Lead who away?" she whispered, suddenly afraid of the answer.

"The ghosts. Nagi sent them to attack me so I would bring them to her."

The wolf must be deranged because Nagi did not send ghosts to attack living creatures. He captured the evil ones after their death if they refused to walk the Way of Souls, forcing them to face judgment.

"Her? The healer you seek is also female?"

"Michaela. She's Niyanoka, like you. The last Seer of Souls and Nagi wants her dead."

Jessie fell back to her seat on the carpet as the possibility of this ricocheted in her brain. Could it be true?

"Why should I believe you?" But she knew why. His black aura, the part that said he had been touched by death. Only a ghost could do that. But it made no sense.

Why would Nagi hunt one of her people and why would a Skinwalker want to protect her? She had been trained from birth to hate the Skinwalkers, to consider them a threat.

His intent blue eyes pinned her. Jessie felt her mouth go dry as she considered the impossible. Could the trickster be speaking the truth? Great Mystery, what evil was this?

She stared in astonishment. There was only one way to find her answers. But she had never even met a Skinwalker before and so did not even know if they dreamed.

But if he dreamed, she would have her chance to learn the truth.

*Look for GHOST STALKER by Jenna Kernan,
available May only from Harlequin Nocturne,
wherever books and ebooks are sold.*

SAME GREAT STORIES AND AUTHORS!

Starting April 2011,
Silhouette Desire will become
Harlequin Desire, but rest assured
that this series will continue to be
the ultimate destination for Powerful,
Passionate and Provocative Romance
with the same great authors that
you've come to know and love!

◆ Harlequin®

Desire

ALWAYS POWERFUL, PASSIONATE
AND PROVOCATIVE

SDHARLEQUIN11